A
LIFETIME
OF
GOODBYES

SAMANTHA TOUCHAIS

Fiction

Copyright Samantha Touchais, 2019
Published by Divinely Inspired Books, 2019

Library of Congress Control Number:2019945909

Print Edition
ISBN-13: 978-0-9969941-2-5
ISBN-10: 0-9969941-2-2

Ebook edition:
ISBN-13: 978-0-9969941-3-2
ISBN-10: 0-9969941-3-0

About the Author

Born in Sydney, Australia, Samantha Touchais has now lived in a total of six countries and has extensively travelled the world for her career in international marketing, as well as to quench her thirst for adventure. Discovering a love and talent for writing in recent years, as well as a passion for helping make the world a more conscious and better place, Samantha has decided to dedicate her time to weaving words into life-changing messages that re-awaken a deeper yearning for meaning in her readers.

She currently lives in Germany with her husband and two young sons.

To my husband.
My dreams have come true because of you.

PROLOGUE

You are about to embark on an adventure. Perhaps not an Indiana Jones-kind of adventure, but it is an adventure nonetheless, and one that happened to me. The living never know what happens when they die, but I discovered that we have a wonderful opportunity to review our lives one more time before we pass over. I was given two days to say goodbye to the life I had built for myself and only two short days to reflect on and review what I had considered to be a life well lived.

I ask you to read my words with an openness of heart as well as mind. There are many messages in this book that I want to share with you, dear reader, and while I can no longer do anything with the lessons I have learned, I am hoping that I can touch the lives of those still living, and help them to see that life is a gift to be enjoyed and cherished and explored. Dare to live, if you will.

Here is my story.

CHAPTER 1

Decisions

THEY SAY YOUR life flashes before your eyes when you die. I always thought that sounded a bit strange because I couldn't really see how a whole life that had been stitched together piece by piece, could just blink and be gone. And while my life didn't flash by, I have been given the opportunity to say goodbye to it, person by person, until I then walk off into whatever is next.

We all fear death, but really it's nothing like I imagined. I feel great! No pain, no concerns, but a wonderful sense of lightness and a shifting level of consciousness that I can't quite figure out yet. It's really rather pleasant, in an odd kind-of-a-way.

Everybody has regrets in life. Some people wear them like a great big fur coat that they never take off, while others shrug their shoulders and throw them to the ground for someone else to pick up. I chose to live a simple life as I thought simple would be safe. Simple would mean no great challenges and therefore no real opportunity for regret or disappointment. But here I am, no longer living but more alive than ever, finally free of the worries and concerns I had carried with me in this life, and I am facing a last chance. 'Last chance' sounds a bit drastic, and I am not one for drama, but simply and plainly, this is what it is.

You see, as I am no longer technically alive, I cannot communicate with anyone. I know this because I found myself on the 204 bus heading to the park where I used to feed the ducks every morning, and I couldn't find my ticket. I approached the driver to see about purchasing another and he completely ignored me! He just stared ahead and no matter how hard I tried to get his attention he just would not respond. So I went to sit down and on gets a rather well-fed lady who nearly sits on me! I leapt out of the way just in time and despite my protests, she ignored me too! It was when she heaved her enormous shopping bag up on the seat where I was sitting, and the BAG WENT RIGHT THROUGH ME, that I realised what must have happened.

I'm getting rather excitable but it really was the most peculiar experience that I haven't quite recovered from yet.

But with instinct and purpose accompanying me on the way home, I knew what I had to do.

There's nothing like dying to sharpen the mind. I had let mine get somewhat dull lately and thought that crossword puzzles would help but they only ever succeeded in sending me to sleep. But my wits had found me again and so I sat down on the bench in our garden and thought about who I wanted to visit one more time.

I never really had a lot of friends. Frivolity is a pet peeve of mine, and I found throughout the years that a lot of friendships were based on trips to the pub or watching sports games. I never saw the point really, and so the few friendships I had in my younger days I slowly let drift away. My wife's very sociable, so we always had people coming and going in our house and the occasional dinner party or barbeque to attend. I never really enjoyed them but I'm a traditional kind-of-a-man and wanted to show good social graces.

But my idea of a good weekend was sitting down with a hot cup of tea and opening up a crisp fresh newspaper to get up-to-date with the local and world affairs. I would then put on my overalls and go and tinker with my vintage car, lovingly taking the dust cover off and admiring her beautiful shape.

Everybody takes their car everywhere these days, and they wonder why the air is so polluted? I'm not one of those environment types, but when we have a perfectly respectable public transportation system, why not use it?

Driving is for sport and pleasure not for sitting in traffic jams stuck behind buses that could have just as easily taken them where they wanted to go. Driving is a privilege and a pleasure and something that I took very seriously.

So I would pick up my gloves and feel the leather stretch and creak as it moulded to my hands in a familiar way. My hat would come out of its box and I would slowly and lovingly lower it on to my head. I didn't need a hat as I was still the proud owner of a thick head of hair, but it's part of the tradition so on it would go.

There's a certain smell that comes from old leather seats, and I savoured that first moment when I opened the door of the car after a week of her sitting in the garage. That familiar welcoming and comforting smell. I had been driving this car for so many years that the seat fitted me perfectly. The engine would start with a small moment's hesitation and then would purr to life, like a cat waking from a luxurious day time nap.

Alas, I will not be able to drive her anymore, and I don't know what will happen to her, as my wife never learned to drive and has no use for her. But death brings with it a certain perspective change and with that an ability to view things from a distance. This doesn't dull the experience but allows us to love without holding on too tightly to anything. To appreciate without obsession which opens up a new level of experience and takes away fear. Fearing loss seems so unnecessary to me now.

I've lived a good life. While it was not an extraordinary or particularly memorable life it was one I am quite content to look back on. Do I have regrets? Of course. But I found myself a good woman to marry, we had two beautiful children and I was able to fulfil my role of husband and father to the best of my abilities. I wouldn't say I have any great achievements to be proud of, but why must one stand out from the crowd? All this self-obsessed culture these days is really rather baffling! Why do people splash their lives around for everyone to see, opening themselves up to criticism while searching for approval? I never really worried about what people thought of me. I wasn't popular at school, and I certainly had my fair share of run-ins with bullies, but with age comes experience and with experience comes wisdom, and I discovered that bullies are really people who are not comfortable in their own skin. They try to re-direct their pain onto someone else, as if pain is something that can be packaged up and thrown to another to catch, so that they don't have to deal with it anymore.

I worked at the same company for forty-five years. Forty-five years! Now that is an achievement I suppose. Young people these days might find that rather boring, but there is a great sense of security that comes from knowing what lies ahead. That may seem dull to some people, to get up every day and to put on the same shirt and tie and head off to the same office, but I'm not one to push myself outside my comfort zone. I like to be in the driver's seat so-to-speak and know what each day will bring.

Did I ever wonder what life could be like if I tried something different? Of course I did, but I suppose I let fear hold me back. I thought I was doing the right thing by focusing on the steady pay check my job provided and after a few years I couldn't see myself doing anything else. I suppose I came to define myself through my job rather than on a deeper level. I can see that now and it gets me wondering what life would have been like had I dared to live my dream life rather than the life I thought I should live.

As I sit here on the bench, I notice the handprints of my children in the concrete path leading to the gate. They were so little when I laid that cement. I remember trying to stretch out my daughter's fingers so that her hand would go evenly into the wet ground but it took a few goes. I lost my temper with her because she wasn't listening to my instructions but I don't think she really understood. At that age everything is a game. I could tell she liked the feeling of the wet cement as it ran over her fingers. She didn't know, couldn't know, that it would dry soon and how special it would be to see her little handprint all these years later. Young children don't seem to have the same concept of time. It is now or yesterday. There is no future to worry about. They have complete and utter trust in the world and in their parents, never questioning or thinking about what could happen, good or bad.

My son used to love throwing himself off the brick wall in our garden. He would land with a thud in the grass and each time my wife would call out to him to be careful. She would watch him from the kitchen window muttering under her breath how it was all going to end in tears. It rarely did but there were definitely a few scrapes and bruises on a regular basis.

Luckily we never had to make any visits to the emergency ward for broken bones. We seemed to get through childhood relatively unscathed. It's rather a miracle really considering how active our children could be.

We didn't escape the hospital altogether though, and there were a few emergency trips on weekends when the GP's office was closed. Our kids never seemed to get sick during office hours. Oh and that dreadful time when my son Benjamin decided to experiment with peas and his sister's ear. They had both been in a silly mood that day and when it came time to sit still at the table for dinner, they both seemed to have ants in their pants. I have little tolerance when it comes to children and dinner tables, and I had quite a few stern words to say that evening. However, as my wife and I were discussing the day's affairs, the children suddenly went silent. Benjamin was looking intently at his plate and Alice was sitting there gaping like a fish.

'My ear feels funny,' she said. 'I can't hear very well.'

'What have you done?!' I demanded while looking directly at Benjamin. 'What have you done?!' I demanded again, grabbing his arm for attention.

'I, I… I… nothing!' he stammered.

Alice had been fiddling with her ear this whole time, and my wife jumped up from the table, pulled Alice's hair back and tried to look inside her ear.

'She has a pea in her ear!' my wife screeched. 'I can't get it out!'

So off we went to the emergency ward to join the countless other parents and children, waiting quietly for snuffly noses, tummy aches and broken bones to be fixed. It was a Sunday night, everyone was tired and it was the last place anyone wanted to be. Oh how I could have strangled Benjamin! Luckily for him my wife had decided to stay home with Benjamin while I took Alice to the hospital. There was no point in us all being there.

The pea was eventually removed and given back to Alice in a plastic bag (she wanted to show her friends at preschool the next day). When we got home, Benjamin came to us with head down and looking all forlorn. I was too tired to say anything more on the matter, so both children were washed, teeth brushed and were sent to bed.

Ah children. Nothing is more stressful nor more perfect than being a parent. Who could have thought that such little people could cause such big trouble but there you have it. Each night I would tuck their tiny bodies into bed, pulling the blankets up around their ears so that their small faces poked out, looking even smaller than they ever did running around during the day. I would kiss them each on their forehead, tell them to sleep well and I would slowly walk out of their room.

If ever anyone was sick during the night, or had woken from a bad dream, it was my wife who would go to them. I had to work the next day and I needed my rest. If I think about it now, I suppose she was working too, running the household and what not, but men just didn't think like that in those days.

I'm glad we had the life that we had together. We were a happy family and while I wasn't always the most patient of fathers, I loved my children very much, and still do.

People are starting to come home from work now. It's that

time of day where we transition from one world to another. Where coats are hung up on hallway racks, slippers gently slipped on to tired feet and families prepare to sit down to a nice hot meal and to discuss the day's events. It's where energy shifts from work life to family life, where the wife is expected to look after the husband when he walks in the door. I think things have changed, what with women entering the work force. I don't really know how young families manage these days. A lot of rushing around, short cuts and stress I suppose.

I hear my neighbour's key enter his front door and I know who I will visit first.

CHAPTER 2

The Neighbour

WE HAVE LIVED next door to each other for forty years but as I walk through his front door for the first time, I realise that I never took the time to get to know my neighbour. Even after George's wife died, I was always too busy to see if he wanted to share a cup of tea together and simply talk about the weather. I kept telling myself I was too busy but now I know I was scared. Scared of having to face raw human emotions. Scared of having to deal with death and despair. It was easier to just keep up the premise of an over-the-fence friendship by waving hello every morning and throwing a 'How's it going?' at him before walking out my gate and down the road to the number 204 that took me to work every morning, and that lately had been taking me to the park to feed the ducks.

As I step over the threshold, I notice photos on the walls in his hallway. One photo in particular catches my eye. It is my neighbour in Egypt standing in front of the pyramids. He is looking rather pleased with himself and is holding a shovel in one hand and handkerchief in the other. I suppose it is hot in Egypt.

I continue down the hallway and I find George feet up on the coffee table watching the television. I excuse myself as I walk in front of him to take the spare seat next to him on the sofa. He lets out a snort of laughter that makes me jump. He is watching one of those silly game shows where the contestants make fools of themselves jumping all over the set trying to catch as much money as they can as it falls from the sky. George clearly finds this amusing but as I look at his face, really look for the first time ever, I notice a sadness in his eyes. The ad break comes on and he leans back into the sofa and stares blankly at the screen waiting for his show to come back on. There is something in his expression that I can't quite place. A certain loneliness perhaps?

I get up and cross over the room to his bookshelf. I see titles of adventure, a few of romance (his wife's I suppose?) and some well-known detective novels lining the shelf. But several books jump out at me. 'The Dummies' Guide to Archaeology,' 'How to dig for Dummies,' and 'Archeology 101.' I feel taken aback. Here I was living next to someone all these years and I never knew we shared a passion. I say passion, but really for me it was a closet interest that never came off the hanger. Archaeology always fascinated me, particularly when I saw a re-run of *Secret of the Incas* at the cinema. Something changed in me the day I saw that movie. My curiosity was piqued and I felt suddenly inspired. I have always had a fascination with history, and being rather good with a shovel, as my garden would attest to, I thought I could combine these interests and skills and become an archeologist. I remember that feeling of pure joy and possibility as I headed home after the cinema and proudly announced to my father that I had found my calling. I will never forget the look on his face. He screwed up his nose and with a voice higher than usual and certainly louder, said 'Archeologist? What preposterous nonsense.' And that was that.

It's a shame to never pursue one's dreams. I realise that now. But I traded a life of discovery for a life of certainty and as I stand here looking at my neighbour's bookshelf I realise what a loss that was.

I can't say I regret the decisions I made in life, and my life turned out rather well, but what if I'd just had that little bit of courage to push myself outside my comfort zone and try something I really loved? My job at the firm was great, and I loved working with numbers. Numbers are clean. They are easy to understand. They don't talk back, and they certainly don't lie. You could manipulate them to a certain extent, add a twist to the interpretation of statistical results, but numbers are numbers and ultimately, they represent the facts.

I never really had the courage to go after my dreams. I suppose I should have taken that first step towards something small and built up from there. I fancied myself a bit of a writer but each time I tried to put pen to paper there would be that familiar voice telling me I was a nobody and what did I have to write about? What life experiences could I draw upon and what great tragedy had befallen me that would lend itself to the drama and suspense that is needed for a good book? I wrote a few poems in my younger years but I never shared them with anybody. I eventually burned them for fear that someone would find them and expose me. I was at a vulnerable stage of my life back then and writing seemed to help me find my voice.

But who would want to read what I had written? Someone once said that we all have one good book inside us, and I'm certain that's true, but I could never quite get over the feeling that I was an imposter. I had no right to think I could possibly write a book.

Writing wasn't encouraged in my day. It wasn't seen in our family as a sustainable profession and I suppose my family were right. We have to take responsibility for our lives, get a good job, earn a good living. Well that's what I used to think. I wonder now whether this was the right path to take. Why can't we play out our dreams while being paid for it? What would it be like to wake up each morning and bounce out of bed knowing you were going to make a difference that day? Surely true happiness is found in the pursuit of our dreams? Someone once said that we create our own reality and I have never really understood that until now. I simply let life happen to me a lot of the time and I now realise what a mistake that was. I see now that we have a choice, but a lot of us live on automatic pilot, never questioning and just doing. Never reflecting but just going about our day in a half daze, physically doing one activity while mentally thinking about another.

What if we stopped once in a while and just dreamed? Let our minds wander where they wanted while being an observer. Listening to our inner guidance, our intuition. It feels strange to talk about this now as this is not how I lived my life, and certainly not what I believed in when I was alive, but I see now that I could have lived a richer life if I had opened my heart and mind to what I was supposed to hear.

It was intuition that led Einstein to his theory of relativity. It was his ability to suspend belief that allowed him to see beyond the current and to the possible, sometimes taking him years to find ways to help others catch up to him. Taking complex ideas such as quantum mechanics and sharing them with the masses was never going to be easy but he followed his inner voice and was never afraid to believe.

Now I don't want to compare myself to Albert Einstein but there is a lesson in there for all of us. If we could suspend our scepticism and disbelief for just a moment, what doors would we open, what ideas would come to us?

I'm getting a bit philosophical which was not my intention, but I am realizing now that life is not all we see. It's how we get from what we see to what we want to see, but don't yet see, that adds another dimension to the everyday, another layer of colour. It's the belief in the unknown and the possible that can transform us, that can lead us in a new and better direction if we only dare.

I sit back down next to George who is leaning forward again watching as the next person scrambles over a rotating barrel while trying to collect £100 bills in a bucket. I look at the lines on his face that appear and disappear only to reappear again when he laughs. His teeth I notice are slightly stained and yet I see no sign of tobacco. Perhaps he smoked in his younger years? Who is this man I sit next to? What dreams did he not fulfil? What fantasies was he too afraid to go after? Did fear of failure hold him back? Fear of disapproval? Disappointment? A lack of self-belief?

And I wonder why I didn't take the time to discover a shared passion? I imagine the kind of friendship we could have had, the commonalities we shared, and I think about the fact that I never took the time to say more than a few niceties to him as I rushed about my life seemingly content to remain within my own four walls. What did I miss out on?

It's funny how you can live next door to someone for forty years and never really know them.

George yawns suddenly, he stretches his arms above his head and then places his hands on his stomach. 'It's time to feed you,' he says as he stands up and walks down the hall towards the kitchen. He opens the fridge door and stands in front of the half-empty shelves, staring for a few seconds as if faced with too much choice.

I look over his shoulder and I can see a small pile of ready-meals for one and a few cans of diet lemonade. But there's nothing comforting in there. No soul food as they call it these days. Why didn't I bring him a meal from time to time? Or better yet, invite him around on the odd occasion? It must have been terribly lonely since his wife died. My wife's an excellent cook and she could have whipped something up for him without much effort. My wife volunteered for Meals on Wheels once the children left home. She would bake a hot dish once a week and deliver single portions to the elderly people living in our neighbourhood. I don't know why I didn't think to slip one next door once in a while. We worry about those we don't know while forgetting to take care of our own backyard. We read about people who died in their apartments but aren't discovered for weeks as no-one ever visited them. I'm feeling a bit morbid now and I don't mean to lower the mood, but it's food for thought.

George carefully chooses a meal, closes the fridge and takes it over to the kitchen bench. He peels back the plastic cover and places the box in the microwave, pressing the instant start button three times. He grabs a glass from the cupboard, returns to the fridge and takes a can of lemonade out. As he pours the contents into his glass, I appreciate another thing about my neighbour; no drinking straight from the can for him! The microwave beeps, he removes his steaming hot dish, and together with his lemonade returns to the TV. As he sits down with a sigh and places a tray on his lap, I decide to remain with him while he eats his meal. At least tonight he will not eat alone.

He finishes his meal, wipes his mouth and places the tray down next to him on the sofa. He continues to stare at the screen as a way to get through the lonely evening before going to bed. It is my time to leave now and as I stand up in front of him, I wish him a happy life. I ask that he is not lonely, that he lives out the rest of his years pursuing the dreams he was always too afraid to go after. I wish for him a life filled with good companionship and connection to others and perhaps another dig or two before his knees give out and arthritis moulds around his fingers.

He suddenly yawns, stretches and pushes himself to standing. He turns off the television and slowly shuffles out of the room. I accompany him as far as the hall and we part ways as George heads towards the kitchen again. I turn and walk out of the house, throwing one last glance towards the photos on the wall. The sun has set and the day has come to a close.

As I head back out through the front gate, I think about who I want to see next, and as I need time to think I turn back towards my house, head down the side path and into the backyard.

I sit down on one of the swings that we installed in our garden when the children were young and then decided to keep in the hope that we would one day become grandparents. I think back over all the fond memories I have of pushing one or the other in the swing, to their squeals of delight and to 'go higher'. The frame would wobble precariously as their little bodies were pushed high up into the air, bottoms bouncing in seats as they reached the peak. What simple yet wonderful memories!

I have a great view of the backs of nearly all the houses in my part of the street from the swing set. Our house is in the middle of a long row of terraced houses, built in the 1920s and all at least two storey. A few people have extended up into the roof over the years, and several have added conservatories at the back but there is still a conformity to the houses that I find reassuring. I watch as one by one the neighbours turn their bedroom lights off, ready to rest and recuperate as they head slowly into the next day.

Having lived on this street for so many years, I feel I know the history of it probably better than anyone! We have seen such changes on this street as young families would come and go, or people would grow old and have to move out of what was often the only home they had ever known, to move into a one-room suite in an old-age facility. I told my wife that I never wanted to do that, never wanted to leave our home and that if necessary, I would move our bedroom downstairs so that we could live a one-level existence while not having to battle the stairs. I always wanted to be surrounded by comfort and the familiar as I got older, but now I don't need to make that decision.

When we first moved into this street it was filled with what I would call like-minded people. We were all from a similar walk of life with similar beliefs and ways of living. We were a tight-knit community and one in which we were able to always lean on each other. But as the London property prices started to rise, and didn't seem to be slowing down, people gradually started expanding out our way, bringing with them a different way of life. I remember when an Indian family moved into the street, and how suspicious everyone was of them. Looking back, I don't know why we felt that way, but after years of living one way it is not always easy to change. Concerns were raised over the smells that would come from their kitchen as they cooked their foreign food, or over the kind of influence their children may have on ours. Those concerns that come out of nothing but racism and a fear of something different.

There was a knock on the door one day and my wife opened it to a smiling woman dressed in a layering of incredible material, covered in sequins and really rather beautiful. The woman introduced herself as Geetha and said she had brought some homemade Indian desserts as a special treat for our family. As my wife took the foil-wrapped package and offered a warm thank you and welcome, I was struck by how brave I thought this woman was. Surely she had picked up on the animosity towards her and her family, the fact that her neighbours didn't want them to be here. Surely she had seen the curtains be quickly and not-so-discreetly pulled aside as her neighbours stared at her as she walked down the street past their houses. And yet here she was offering us a glimpse of her generosity and openness and capacity for acceptance and forgiveness that one could not help but admire.

As we shared the treats with our children that night after dinner, I remarked to my wife on the ability for food to bring people together, how it can be used as an introduction to another world, as a key to open a door into a different realm. How the offering of a home-cooked meal can mean so much to someone. It's a true sign of love and of a big heart.

I look up suddenly as I see the light in a nearby house turn on and see a young mother with a babe in arms stand at the window looking out. I don't know this young lady very well, as they only moved into the house a few months ago just before their baby was born, and I feel her loneliness reach out and grab me as she looks for any signs of life other than her baby's.

It was a very rare occasion that I would be up during the night with one of our kids when they were very young, but the odd time when my wife needed to rest, and a baby called out, I always found it an extremely lonely experience. I would long to be back in my bed, warm and safe, and I would feel quite vulnerable being up in the middle of the night with only a young and completely helpless baby for company. I used to look out the window to see if anyone was also up at this time, and I took great comfort on the odd occasion when I would see a neighbour's light on. I wouldn't feel so alone then.

As I look back at the young mother's house, I see another light turn on out of the corner of my eye. I turn my head towards the other end of the street and see the light in old Mrs Morcombe's kitchen go on, as she most likely was up during the night making herself a warm cup of milk to help her go back to sleep. Two people at very different stages of life but both up during the night wishing they could be back in bed asleep.

Our street has seen its own share of heartaches too. We were all affected by the situation with the family in number 56. A nasty divorce led to a very stressed-out single mother, who was not able to cope with the hand she had been dealt. My wife used to see her on the school run, and while they got on well, and my wife said she was a very nice lady who was really very kind, gradually my wife started to pull away from her, not knowing how to cope with her negativity.

Our daughter went to play at her house one day, as she was friends with one of her daughters from school, but when she came home she begged not to go back there. She said the house was a mess and the four animals that lived inside left a terrible smell. She seemed really affected by her visit and so my wife said that she didn't have to go back. We would invite the little girl to our house from time to time to give her mother a break, and to give the little girl a break from her older sister, who also was not coping very well with their change in circumstance.

One day we noticed flashing blue lights reflecting in our living room and when we looked out, we saw two police officers heading into the house. They remained inside for a good half an hour or so, and then headed outside again, turned off the blue flashing lights and left. After much hesitation my wife decided to go down and knock on the door and see if everything was alright.

She came back an hour later, absolutely drained and quite upset. She said that the ex-husband had apparently called the police claiming the mother was mistreating the girls, in what the mother believed was a pure act of vengeance. To mess with the lives of children like that was truly disgusting! I admit the house was unclean, and the mother had lost the ability to manage the older girl's aggression towards herself and the younger sister, but that surely didn't require a visit from the police. Worse, she was to be closely followed by the Department of Child Protective Services to ensure that the claims of mistreatment were untrue.

As I was listening to my wife re-telling the story, I could not imagine what it must be like to have someone in your house judging your every move and your every interaction with your child. I do understand the need for this interception at times, but having it happen to our neighbour really brought the situation home to us. Parents are judged enough as it is but to be judged with the objective of perhaps having one's children taken away from them, I cannot even relate to.

The situation deteriorated even further between this poor woman and her ex-husband, so much so that my wife offered to take the girls for the afternoon several times per week to give the overwhelmed mother a break. But soon this offer started to be abused, with my wife coming home one day after an outing with our children to find the neighbour's two girls sitting on our doorstep. They said they had been there since mid-afternoon and it was now close to five, and that they were there because their mother said she needed a break. My wife was horrified and called up the mother asking for an explanation. She didn't answer the phone and when my wife took the girls back to their house, there was no-one to answer the door.

The girls had dinner with us that night and as they were heading into Alice's bedroom to play we heard a knock at the door. It was the girls' mother. My wife took her into the living room and closed the door so that the children wouldn't hear them talking.

When they emerged, the mother looked a bit shaken, but as she waited for the girls to answer her call to go home, she thanked my wife again for all she had been doing. She said that things were very hard for her and that she desperately needed a break. She said the ex-husband was supposed to have the girls the following week and that she was really looking forward to the time alone. She said she was sick of dealing with all the hassles that the girls created and just wanted time to herself.

All this was said in front of her two young daughters as they came down the stairs to say their goodbyes.

I do not want to judge this woman, and she certainly had been having a very tough time, with an equally difficult ex-husband to deal with, but children are innocent of adult situations, and should be kept that way. The fact that this mother didn't seem concerned that her daughters had heard this conversation was what bothered my wife and me the most.

A few weeks later, my wife received a very tearful and panicked call. It was the neighbour again, and she said she had just been to see her lawyer who had announced to her that the girls were to be temporarily taken away by the Department of Child Protective Services. My wife was asked if she would be a character witness, to which she begrudgingly agreed. The case was to be heard the following month, and my wife was to comment truthfully on what she had observed with the mother and her children. My wife didn't sleep in the nights leading up to the case. She was so concerned about what would happen to the girls and couldn't imagine children being taken away from their mother. In those days, children were not normally sent to live with the father, and so their fate lay somewhere between a distant relative in another town or a foster home.

We discussed the situation many times together and finally agreed that the best thing she could do was tell the truth, which was that the mother was always physically there for the girls but not emotionally. While she never missed a school concert or sports day, she had lost the ability to speak kindly to her children and treated them like a pain in her side. She either didn't realise, or chose to ignore, the fact that children build their self-belief systems on what they hear from those they love and admire, and a mother's words were sacred to a child. All these girls seemed to hear from their own mother was that they only caused trouble for her and that her life was much better when they weren't around.

My wife was certain that this was not the case, but if a mother doesn't know how to speak to her child with kindness and love, the child will absorb the negativity little by little, learning to believe that they are worthless and are not worth loving. This can only lead to trouble later on, and I believe is a leading cause of drug-use and teenage pregnancies.

My wife came home from court on the day of the trial shaken and with a headache. She was pale and I told her to go to bed and that I would look after the children, see them bathed and fed and put to bed. She said all she wanted to do was to hold her children close to her and to keep them safe and to tell them how much she loved them.

Our neighbour didn't end up losing the girls, but the situation shook the whole street to the core. We will never really know what went on in that house, how alone the girls often were while their mother was emotionally disengaged from them. They moved out of the street the following year and we lost touch with them. I really hope that they managed to find their feet as a family and that the mother was able to get the support from her family that the move was intended to provide.

One always assumes that one knows someone based on so little, just a few simple facts and figures with a sprinkling of gossip. But one never knows what goes on behind closed doors. We use facts and figures to separate people but then life brings them back together. I think about the young mother and the old lady up together in the night due to a shared situation of no sleep. I realise how we all share struggles in life and that we are not so different from how we like to think we are. If only we could recognise these similarities rather than focusing on the differences.

As the sun slowly starts to come up in the sky, and the birds stretch sleepy wings and sing to their families and neighbours to welcome them to the new day, I think about how I have allowed myself to remain separate from people, and how I never valued relationships with others perhaps as much as I should have. As I walk back up the side path and towards the street, I know who I want to visit next and I turn towards my best friend Harold's house.

CHAPTER 3

The Best Friend

I'VE KNOWN HAROLD for as long as I can remember. We met when we were in Boy Scouts together and fast became firm friends. We certainly had our ups and downs, and finding that Harold was slightly too competitive for my taste, I drifted away from him during our teenage years. But when university rolled around, we found ourselves enjoying a firm friendship once again, one that lasted the rest of our lives.

Male friendships are funny things. They are certainly not like the kinds of friendships I saw my wife share with her close group. From the day we are born, men are supposed to compete with each other; compete in sport, compete for the girl, compete for the job. From my experience, male friendships are not based on outpourings of emotions, and always seemed a bit shallow to me. If I can be so bold as to say, I believe that men probably have less true friends than women, but the friendships we do form we tend to value, although we would never admit that to anyone!

Due to the competitive side of the male nature, I think a true male friendship can only be formed amongst equals, otherwise the alpha male tries to take over, which completely changes the dynamics. While I sampled a few friendships over the years, there was really only one person I was able to maintain a true connection with. The rest I let go of. That one person was Harold. I start to think about him again, and as people now have finished their cups of morning coffee and their rushed breakfasts and are starting to get ready for work, I know that if I hurry I can join Harold on his early morning walk.

As I head around the corner of the street he still lives on with his wife and two cats (his son left home long ago), I nearly bump into him. He seems to side-step me slightly, although perhaps that was my imagination. I turn around and quickly try to keep up. Harold was diagnosed with diabetes a few years ago, and to his credit he has put in an enormous effort to change his ways. He drastically changed his diet, very quickly losing the belly fat he had been working hard to build up all these years, and he took up walking. I must admit I had a little chuckle to myself the first time I saw him dressed up in his walking gear. He had a sweat band around the top of his forehead, and a towel around his neck, his large glasses bobbing up and down with the rhythm of his walking. His enormous belly was straining against his tracksuit and as he walked he pumped his arms, puffed his cheeks in and out and had such a look of determination on his face that no-one dared laugh at him.

As I join him now, I admire the restraint he showed after his diagnosis and the man I now see before me. He has lost the sweatband and his clothes aren't as tight any more, but he still walks with a serious look of steely determination on his face which is quite impressive.

As our feet pound the pavement my mind starts to wander, and I find myself thinking back to the time he chose to open up to me about his marriage. It took me very much by surprise as that is not the sort of friendship we had, but I suppose that he felt he could trust me after knowing each other practically most of our lives. I had been his best man at his wedding and had known his wife almost as long as he had.

He asked me to join him at the pub (my least favourite place to be!) saying that he needed my advice, and as he went off to get us some drinks, I wondered what on earth he wanted to talk about. I must admit I felt rather uncomfortable as we never shared our feelings with each other, and I didn't think I was really cut out to be in such a position! But I sat up straight as Harold came back to our table and decided that I simply had to try my best.

Harold looked troubled, and as he sat back down at the table, he took a long sip of his beer and then another before he started to speak.

'I've met someone else.' Silence. I simply didn't know what to say.

'I'm sorry?' I asked, not quite believing if I had heard correctly.

Harold's guilt-ridden eyes met mine and he looked like a small child who had stolen an extra piece of chocolate and been caught.

I sat there in silence, staring at him, completely inexperienced with a situation such as this.

'Where did you meet her?' I finally managed to stammer.

'She's a patient in my dental practice. She has really nice teeth!' he said, as if this explained everything.

'Does Geraldine know?' I asked, thinking of his wife.

'No, she doesn't suspect a thing and I don't want her to know. Not yet. I just don't know what to do. I am happy with Geraldine, and we adore our son, but things seem so much fresher when I'm with Marilyn. I seem to be able to forget all my worries when I'm with her.' He fell silent, forlorn eyes looking deep into his beer. As he drained his glass he stood up and said he was going to get another one. I had barely touched mine, not being much of a beer drinker myself, but it was the drink of choice when two men got together to discuss their feelings, or at least that's what I'd seen on the television.

When he sat back down again, I asked Harold what he intended to do.

'That's just it,' he said. 'I don't know! I love my wife but I am starting to have real feelings for Marilyn. She's great fun to be around and we have a good laugh together.'

I built up the courage to ask the question I had been putting off. 'Have you... you know.'

'Oh goodness no! Not yet. I mean I wouldn't do that while I'm still married. That would be cheating and I'm certainly not a cheater!'

As I wrestled with whether I should point out that I thought that having feelings for someone else was still a form of cheating, I looked around the room at the mostly young crowd. There were a few older men sitting at the bar, clearly the regulars, and the rest of the room was filled with the Thursday after-work crowd at one end and the dart players at the other. They all seemed very carefree and oblivious to the weight of the conversation we were having.

'Do you think you will leave Geraldine?' I asked.

'I don't want to. I love her. We have Benji together, but I just can't stop thinking about Marilyn. I wish that somehow I could bring these two worlds together. Have both women in my life, perhaps we could all eventually live together.'

'Stop!' I shouted. 'Listen to what you are saying! You're a married man! I am sure you are not the first married man to have feelings for another woman, and I am sure you won't be the last, but you are married and that is fact. You need to sort yourself out with Geraldine first before having anything to do with Marilyn.' I let out air through my teeth as I sat back in my chair. I took a first proper drink of my beer since this conversation had begun.

'Geraldine thinks Marilyn is quite lovely,' Harold said indignantly.

'What? Wait, she's met her?!' I faltered, barely able to get my words out.

'Well, I may have invited her to dinner recently as she has just moved into the area and didn't know anyone.' Harold said in a quiet voice.

'She's been in your house?!' I exclaimed, my voice starting to find its strength.

'Yes, but Geraldine doesn't know anything about my feelings for her. Oh, what have I done!' Harold looked miserable. I could see that he was completely lost and had no idea which way to go. I didn't know what to say to him at this point in time as I had no experience of what he was facing, and I also couldn't really see how he had got himself into this mess in the first place. One thing was for sure though, and that was that he had to make up his mind fast.

I spoke again. 'Why don't you and Geraldine go away for the weekend and we can have Benji with us? It will do you two good to have some time together and for you to think about how you really feel. I advise not seeing Marilyn anymore until you have sorted out your feelings for Geraldine. Think about it.'

With that, our conversation ended, and I stood up to leave. I thought that Harold would come with me, but he said he was going to stay and finish his beer. He asked me not to say anything to my wife as he didn't want anything to get back to Geraldine. He knew how trustworthy my wife was so I think it was more that he was ashamed of his situation.

As I walked out of the pub, I stepped aside to let a woman walk in, and I felt like I knew her. I had a strong suspicion that it was Marilyn but I decided to give Harold the benefit of the doubt.

The following week Harold called and asked if we could meet again. He said he had been doing a lot of thinking and had come to a decision. We arranged a time and a place and then I nervously put down the phone. I honestly had no idea where his thinking had taken him, and my fear was that his heart was really leading the way and not his head. Marriage can be a tough experience at times, but it shouldn't be taken lightly, and I feared that Harold was not thinking things through enough. He was not just making decisions for himself; there were three other people directly affected by this situation.

I walked into the pub to find Harold seated at the same table as last time, two full pints of beer and one empty in front of him on the table.

'I got you a beer,' he said, getting straight to the point. I took my coat off, placed it over the back of the spare chair next to me and sat down. I picked up the beer with a nervous hand, the glass slipping in my fingers because of the condensation on the outside of it.

'I'm leaving her,' he said, plain and simple.

'Who? Geraldine or Marilyn?' I ventured at last.

'Geraldine. It simply won't work. Every time I am with Geraldine, all I can think about is Marilyn. I see her smiling face everywhere I go. She haunts my dreams and I know I need to be with her.' He shrugged his shoulders as a way of further explanation, as if to say, 'What can I do about it? It's outside of my control.'

My body fell back into the chair and I let out a whistle. I sat there staring at him for a moment while I gathered my thoughts. I knew I had to tread carefully if I was to salvage any of this situation.

'Does Geraldine know? What about Benji?' I asked.

'Geraldine knows, Benji doesn't. We agreed that we will tell him over the weekend when his exams are over. It would be too much for him to take on board right now.' He took another sip of his beer, a storm of emotions rolling across his face.

'Does Marilyn know?' I asked. It seemed like a silly question, but the situation was so surreal I didn't really know how to proceed.

'Yes, of course. She is thrilled! She feels sorry for Benji, and Geraldine of course, but "true love must run its course" as she says.' He took another sip of his beer, not looking fully convinced of what he was saying.

What would I have done in that situation? I really don't know. I would like to take the moral high ground and say that I wouldn't have let it happen in the first place, but Harold was a good guy, a caring guy, he wasn't self-centred or callous. He loved his family, but it appeared he simply wasn't in love with Geraldine anymore. I wonder if that fact had been precipitated by meeting Marilyn or whether he was aware of it all along. But would he ever have left Geraldine if he hadn't met someone else? Who can say how affairs of the heart really work? I don't think it is something one can analyse.

Harold drained his beer and said 'Geraldine is being amazing about the whole thing. She is obviously upset but she knows my mind is made up. We have agreed that I will move out and she has offered to help me find a flat.' He fell silent again.

I couldn't believe what I was hearing! How could she be so understanding? Was that a sign of true love or of complete stupidity? The expression 'If you love someone, set them free' came to mind but I felt a strong urge to resist its meaning.

'Benji really likes Marilyn and Marilyn is great with kids! We will try to have him alternate weekends.' He suddenly put his head in his hands, and I thought he would cry. When he lifted his face, he looked utterly exhausted, the internal battle over the last few months finally wearing him down. I had no idea what to say. This level of conversation was out of my experience, and while we had known each other for most of our lives, it wasn't the sort of conversation we were used to sharing.

'Look, I really don't know what to say', I said, honestly. 'If you need a place to stay for a while, you are always welcome to stay with us, and the offer still stands to take Benji if you two need to discuss matters. I'm sorry that you and Geraldine are separating, and we will ensure we stay friends with both of you, and no hard feelings. I really wish things weren't this way, but I suppose you have made up your mind and you know which direction you are heading in now. At least there's that.' I sighed again, tired and lost in my thoughts.

'You will really like Marilyn, I know you will! She's a great person, very smart. I know you two will get along really well. We should get together soon so you can get to know her.' Harold's face suddenly filled with hope. But I just couldn't give him the approval he was looking for, not at that moment.

'We'll see. I think you and Geraldine need to sort things out and you need to help poor Benji through this first. It will be a huge shock for him and you really need to give him time to get used to the idea. Meeting Marilyn as a friend of yours is one thing, but as the woman you are leaving his mother for is quite another.' I said, surprised by the bitterness in my voice.

'Steady on, I need your support not your judgment!' Harold stated. I could understand that, but I just didn't know how to be there for him. I told him I would do my best to support him, but that I too needed time to get used to the situation. My goal was to help him get through the separation from Geraldine, and then we could talk about my meeting Marilyn. I wanted the best for Harold, and for him to be happy, but there were too many hearts being broken.

A few weeks later we took Benji for the weekend, allowing his parents to get themselves organised. I felt really sorry for the lad, I knew he had a bumpy road ahead of him and that it wouldn't be easy. We had prepared the children and had tried our best to explain what was happening, as the situation affected them too and we wanted them to be sensitive to Benji's needs. We had planned lots of activities for the three of them as we wanted to take Benji's mind off things as much as possible.

Benji's behaviour was atrocious that weekend; he was rude and moody and really very unpleasant to be around. The children found it very difficult as they normally got on well together, but they ended up doing their best to avoid him. By Sunday, we had changed plans and my wife agreed to spend time just with Benji alone and try to give him the support he clearly needed. None of this was his fault and yet he seemed to have blamed himself. My wife worked hard trying to get him to see that he was still very loved but that sometimes marriages don't work out. She told him that his parents would always love him, and they would never stop being his parents, but his family had just changed shape, and he needed to allow himself time to get used to it.

The separation went ahead and Harold moved out. He had hired a van and had asked myself and another friend to help load and unload his things. When we arrived at the flat, I was filled with pity for him. As they had agreed that Geraldine and Benji would remain in the house, there was not much budget for a decent flat and all he could afford was a small, dark and very dingy one. We moved him in and then sat on the old two-seater sofa to have a break and a drink. We saluted his health and his new life with our now-empty water glasses.

About six months later, Harold rang me. He again said he wanted to see me and could we meet at the pub that evening. His voice sounded strained and I wondered what had happened. When I arrived at the pub, he was sitting at the bar, and he waved me over to him. I climbed onto the bar stool and ordered a sparkling water, and then turned to face Harold.

'It's not working out,' he said, defeat written all over his face. 'I thought she was the love of my life, but I think I've made a mistake.' He fell silent.

'Why? What's happened?' I asked, again feeling out of my comfort zone.

'Nothing really, but that initial spark we felt has gone, and now we have fallen into a mundane routine much too quickly for my liking.' As he sighed, I thought about what a mess he was in.

'I think you need to take some time for yourself to really figure out what you want to do,' I said. 'You can't keep stringing everyone along.'

'I'm not trying to!' he rebutted. 'But I am completely confused and am looking for some advice from a friend. You have known me for a very long time and know me almost better than anyone, so I am really hoping that you can tell me what to do!' He slumped down further in his bar stool, utter hopelessness written all over his face.

Again, I felt sorry for him. He was a good guy and was not trying to upset anybody. He was trying to make himself happy, that was all, but unfortunately that small indulgence had turned into something much bigger.

'Dust off your rods and go fishing for the weekend,' I said. 'Alone!' I added as he perked up and was about to invite me. 'You need time away from everybody to think and really try to understand your feelings and what you want to do. You may not end up staying with Marilyn but that doesn't necessarily mean you go running home to Geraldine. Sort yourself out and then we will take it from there,' I said. We agreed to meet again when he had returned from his time away.

A few weeks later, as we sat down to discuss his situation again, he seemed different. He wasn't his usual bright and cheery self, but he seemed lighter than the last time I saw him.

'I've come to a decision again,' he said. 'I did a lot of thinking about Marilyn and tried to really understand how this all started and how we ended up the way we did. I realised that while Marilyn was a breath of fresh air, and we could have fun together, she's not Geraldine. Geraldine and I have been through so much together, and I suppose after so many years of marriage things just got a bit stale. But no one loves me as unconditionally as Geraldine, and I realised that when Marilyn started to try to change me. It was subtle at first but then became quite blatant. We had quite a few fights over it!' He had a beer in hand, as he usually did, but he wasn't relying on it so much this time. I took that as a good sign.

'OK,' I said. 'So you want to call things off with Marilyn, right?'

'Correct,' he said. 'And I want to go back to Geraldine.' He smiled, and I thought *He's gone mad! Why would Geraldine take him back after everything he had put her, and Benji, through?*

'Do you think she'll have you back?' I asked, uncertain of the answer.

'I certainly hope so. Do *you* think she'll have me back?' He looked at me nervously, expectation written all over his face.

'What would you do in her shoes?' I asked. His eyes dropped down to the counter. He didn't speak for a long time, and I let him stay in his silence. He eventually lifted his eyes and said 'I'd probably slam the door in my face, but then again, I'm not Geraldine. She is much more forgiving, and certainly much more understanding, than me. She has always put the family ahead of herself and I really hope she is able to do so this time.' He sighed, again carrying the weight of the world on his shoulders.

I advised him not to say anything to Benji and to again send Benji to us for the weekend while he tried to talk to Geraldine. I prayed she would find the strength to do the right thing, whatever that was. I had no idea what I would do in that situation, but I am pretty sure that my wife wouldn't have been as understanding and accommodating. I know Harold never set out to hurt anybody but how do you move on from something like that? Isn't that the ultimate betrayal, to find someone you supposedly prefer to be with than your own wife or husband? I know that some view monogamous relationships as going against nature, but swans do it, wolves too. If the mate of a swan dies, they never find another one, remaining committed to their partner for the rest of their lives. There's something in that idea, hard as it can feel sometimes.

I am not judging people who choose not to be together any more, certainly not, and having seen many couples around us break up over the years, I know it is not an easy nor pleasant thing to go through. But once an infidelity happens, how do you forgive your partner and take them back? Does the trust ever truly return? Can it? I didn't know the answers to these questions and I am grateful now that I never needed to.

My wife and I had long discussions about the situation between Harold and Geraldine. Of course, we wanted things to work out for them, for their sake and particularly for Benji's, but ultimately Harold needed to accept whatever Geraldine's decision was and move on. Benji needed stability whether than meant living with two parents or one, and Harold couldn't keep changing his mind.

It's so easy for a couple to come apart from each other. Once the initial romance and excitement fades, and routine sets in, it is easy to lose sight of why you fell in love with each other in the first place. Add children to the mix and one can tend to get so caught up in the every day aspects of life, that the couple can forget to talk about their dreams and aspirations. Without realising it one finds oneself drifting away from a shared vision of life and the connection is lost. When the children grow up and move out of home, or retirement starts, suddenly two people together for decades find they now have nothing to talk about. No longer are school discussions necessary, and problems at work no longer exist, and a big cavernous silence takes their place. Two people find themselves looking at each other and trying to remember why they were together in the first place, or worse, discovering that those reasons are no longer valid.

It is so important to always stay connected, to put the effort in from the very beginning. Sure, the working week can be tiring, and sleepless nights with young children exhausting, but it is too easy to slip into a routine that feels comfortable and necessary at the time, but that eventually takes the place of shared dreams and plans for the future. Conversation becomes solely about the children or domestic issues and no longer about each other as individuals. I suppose that is what happened to Harold and Geraldine.

In the end, Geraldine took Harold back. It took a while for them to find their feet again, and Harold said that Benji was quite reserved at first, and very wary that Harold would leave again, but after a while things got back on track. Forgiveness is a truly beautiful and powerful thing and can lead to a lot of happiness if one lets it.

I look at Harold as he marches along the footpath. He's been a good friend to me, as I have to him, and while I didn't really have friends in this life, I think that if anyone was to be my one and only true friend, there was no one better suited than Harold.

'Take care of your family,' I tell Harold one last time. 'Enjoy the years you have left on this earth and really cherish those around you. It's been a real honour knowing you and I'm truly grateful that life has blessed you with happiness and brought you forgiveness.'

I ponder over that final word. Such a simple word to say but it is loaded heavily with meaning. Forgiveness gets me thinking about my brother and I find my legs heading in the direction of the cemetery.

CHAPTER 4

The Brother

THEY SAY YOU can pick your friends but you can't pick your family. Well that is certainly true and I learned that the hard way as I lived through years of an on-again off-again relationship with my brother. That man caused more headaches and more heartbreak than I care to even remember, but he was still my brother and I have often thought about him over the years.

We were never really close. There were only two years between us and I think that created a lot of rivalry that my parents never knew what to do with. One of my first memories is of trying to get rid of him. We had a fish pond in our back garden and John was desperate to have a close look. Well, as any five-year-old would, I jumped on the opportunity to 'help' him, so I told him to stand on my hands and I pushed his little three-year-old body up and over the fence. It was no easy feat, but I was feeling very motivated that day. He landed with a big 'thwack' right in the middle of the pond. I don't remember a splash, but I suppose that was because the pond fence was quite high, and he hit the water with a lot of speed and went right down to the bottom. I indulged in a moment of sweet satisfaction until he came up coughing and spluttering and screaming for our mother. Instincts kicked in and

I knew if I was going to survive this episode I had to think fast. I searched for anything I could use to put against the fence to make it look like he had gone over it himself, but I couldn't find anything. In my panic I took off at great speed with Mother's words of 'WAITTILLYOURFATHERGETSHOME!!!' ringing in my ears.

I got a wholloping that night. My father didn't often lose his temper but when he did it was quite terrifying. I was very sore for several days but not as sore as my poor brother. He really did get a nasty fright but in his sweet and innocent three-year-old way he kept trying to play with me and seemed even more glued to my side than he had been previously. I don't think he realised what happened that day, and I certainly wasn't going to tell him.

As we grew older, we went through the usual fights over toys which later on turned into fights over girls. There was one girl in particular that I secretly liked, and I confessed this to my brother late one night when we were both tucked up in our respective beds but not yet asleep. He took it upon himself the very next day to ask her out, and from that day on I decided I could never trust him again.

As the years went on, we went off on our separate paths, him an architect and me an accountant. As the first-born son I was expected to follow in my father's footsteps whereas my younger brother could do as he pleased. I never fully forgave my parents for what felt like pure favouritism toward my brother, but I suppose when you have your hopes pinned on one son, it takes the pressure off having to pin something on the other.

We spoke on and off over the years and would see each other at Easter and Christmas. When our parents died we drifted apart and didn't put much effort in. I called him the day we found out that we were expecting our first child and I remember being met with silence. He then quickly shared his congratulations and hurried off the phone. I didn't understand why until a few years later when he and his wife announced they were to divorce. They had been trying for a baby themselves and after several miscarriages, one very late in the pregnancy, the stress all got too much, and their marriage broke down. I felt sorry for him that day. He had always been one for keeping up appearances, and so I was shocked to see what a shell of a man he had become.

He came to me one day with a renewed enthusiasm that I hadn't seen in years. He said he had a brilliant business opportunity. One that was too good to pass up. Now, I believe in hard work. I believe that we need to work for things in life and that nothing is given for free. But there was something in his enthusiasm, in his certainty that made me think twice. *Get rich quick schemes don't work*, I kept thinking, and yet his arguments were irrefutable. He had an opportunity to invest in a new mining venture in Africa and all he needed was a small down payment and the rest could be paid in instalments. The opportunities for profit were too large to pass up and all we had to do was sit back and watch our money grow.

Now I should have trusted my gut. God gave us instinct for a reason. But instead I got caught up in his infectious energy and excitement and didn't really think things through. He was my brother after all and if he said he had checked things out thoroughly then I was sure that he had.

So I gave him a large chunk of our savings. Even though I was the accountant, I reasoned that he would take care of the financial side and would ensure that all was above board as he was my brother and was heavily involved in the venture. I even planned for what we would do with the dividends we would receive. We had always wanted to take the children to Disneyland and I thought that by delaying the trip and investing the money we had put aside, we would still eventually be able to take them on their dream trip but also save for their future.

I never saw the money again. Nor the profits. My brother took the money and used it all for himself. He travelled the world, he spent it on women, and he did Heaven-only-knows-what-else with it. It turns out there was no venture. There had been nothing to invest in except his own selfish lies. I had trusted him with my children's happiness, and my children's future, only for him to squander it on nothing.

It took me six months to realise what had happened and by then it was too late. The money was gone and he had no way to pay it back. What do you do? Do you take your brother to court and display all your family's dirty laundry for the world to see? To what end? To punish him for what he did to us? He showed no remorse, he was worth nothing and so going to court would not get back my children's dreams.

I looked at photos of us as children and for the first time truly acknowledged the divide that had always been between us. The divide Mother tried so hard to break down but only succeeded in strengthening. She had always said that all she wanted was for her boys to be close. Her boys were her world and she would do anything to keep us together. But she could not see the damage she was creating. The comparisons she made without reflection. The pressure she placed on me as the older brother to set the example and to be the leader. The advantages she allowed my brother to exploit because he was the baby. He was the charmer. He would look up at Mother with his big soft eyes and tell her what she wanted to hear. He needed her. He made her feel wanted.

I, on the other hand, was 'too independent'. I was too capable and didn't need her for the little things that were so big for her. Isn't that the goal of a parent, to create a child who is independent of the parent? Who can survive independently in this world and make a success of their life? Isn't that what animals do? They don't seem to question their role as parents, they do what comes naturally and when it is time for their young to grow up and move on wouldn't they celebrate a job well done? Why do we put so much of our own dreams and desires onto our children? Why do we judge them for what they choose to become when it doesn't align with the dreams we had for ourselves?

I felt very judged by my parents. No, not my parents, my

mother. But not knowing how to handle her, my father would often side with her and push the blame on to me. So while I was expected to be the older and therefore the wiser of the two brothers and to set the good example that he needed to follow, I was also expected to be dependent and vulnerable and in need of my mother which I never managed to reconcile.

I digress but I realise now that I held a lot of resentment towards my brother, even from a young age. I felt that I carried all the hopes and expectations on my shoulders and he was free to be himself and to be the golden child who could do no wrong. He waved to me from outside the boundaries that I was confined by. He was free to roam in the fields and chase dreams and butterflies while I had to stay inside the fence and look after the proverbial homestead.

I accepted this role initially with grace. I allowed myself to be moulded into the big responsible brother, into the creator of close family ties. But when I fully embraced this role and allowed it to speak to who I was becoming as a person, Mother questioned me and became disappointed in me, as I no longer relied on her. The person I had been shaped to be quickly became unacceptable. What was I to do? What could I have done? I chose to remain in this role as it was as much a part of me as the air I was breathing. Meanwhile my brother seemed to know what Mother wanted and seemed to be able to superficially shape himself to her needs. I watched as they became closer and closer and as I became more distant. The close brotherly bond my mother wanted so badly for us was slowly and carefully being pulled down brick by brick.

One day I found myself standing face to face with the man who had betrayed me. Who had literally taken my money and run. We were at the airport both about to board planes but for different reasons; him to go off on another adventure, me to go to the funeral of an old family friend. I managed a few words that I don't remember, feeling the bile rise in my throat. I wanted to punch him. I felt such anger. He just smiled. My fists closed into tight balls and my throat constricted. Why did he seem to float through life, why did life give him no consequences to face? How could he not care? Our mother had died several years before and he barely made it to the funeral. He had been trekking through Thailand and had not been reachable. He begrudgingly boarded a plane to come home for the funeral and was gone again the next day. Good old reliable me was left to pick up the pieces. The responsible older child was asked yet again to step into shoes clearly too big for the younger brother to fill.

The bitterness took me by surprise, but it was to be expected. 'How could you,' was all I could stammer. It wasn't a question as I knew there would be no answer. How could you answer for a betrayal such as his? My children flashed before my eyes. The day we had to tell them that we no longer had the money to take them on their dream trip, their little faces crumpled and all I could do was thank God my brother had not been close by at that moment.

So here I was before him, his face calm and completely guilt-free. He said he had to go as he needed to board his plane. I stood there frozen by anger and bitterness and bile. I watched his back retreat and I barely breathed. When I could no longer see him, I took a deep breath and walked to my gate where I half sat half collapsed into the seat. Why is it that the best comebacks occur after the person has walked away? I had so many things I wanted to say to him all of a sudden, but it was too late. I thought them anyway as I stared at the bright blue carpet and the pieces of old chewing gum that had been trampled further and further in to the ground. *That's like me* I thought, with a strange half smile on my lips. *I've allowed too many people to do this to me but no more.* I resolved I would no longer think about my brother. I would erase him from my memory. I would recreate happy memories, ones where I could just be, no responsibilities and just a normal happy childhood. One where I wasn't exploited and twisted and manipulated all for the supposed good of the family. It took me a while but eventually I was able to let go. I never forgave though.

Standing before his grave now I realise what a ball of bitterness I have been carrying with me all these years. We had had some fun times growing up. I admired the way he could let himself go and be completely carefree. He had an infectious laugh which is why people loved him so much. They couldn't help smiling when he was around. They felt good. I was the serious older brother who carried the weight of the world on his shoulders. People didn't laugh so much with me. What if I had learned to be a little bit like him? Sure, that wasn't allowed or encouraged during our childhood but why did I let those years define me so much as an adult? Why did I let him affect me so much? I suppose when your children are involved it is hard not to react, not to take things to heart. You are the keeper of their hearts when they are little, and when someone breaks through that protective wall you feel you have let everyone down and you resolve to never let that happen again. But what if I had chosen to forgive him? What would that have meant?

We view forgiveness as something we do for the other person, but actually it is the ultimate act of self-care. Forgiving someone is not the same as saying that what that person did was OK. Forgiveness can be a way of saying to that person that they can no longer hurt you. You are giving them back what they did to you as it is now their burden to carry. You can forgive in many ways, and it really depends on the depth of the hurt and the closeness to that person, but I could have forgiven my brother I realise now. Forgiving him at the time felt like I was letting myself and my children be vulnerable again, and there was no way I was going to do that. But I could have forgiven him without letting him back in my life. Forgiving him would not have absolved him of his sins. I truly don't think he would have cared either way. He didn't need my forgiveness and he certainly wasn't seeking it. But what if I had chosen to let go of the feelings he had pushed me to create? What if I had imagined a conversation with him where I told him that while I didn't agree with what he had done, I forgave him because he didn't realise the depth of hurt he had created? What if I had been able to say that I no longer wanted to carry the guilt for destroying my children's dream, for making them cry. That was his guilt to do with what he wanted, but it no longer infected our family. It no longer belonged to me. I was no longer its carrier. The relief would have been enormous.

So as I stand staring at his gravestone, I do the ultimate act of self-love. I tell him that I fully forgive him for what he did to me and my family. For the years of injustices that I suffered at his hands. For the manipulations he had made of our family and in particular of our mother.

I always wondered what our mother would have said about the money. I'm sure she would have found a way to defend him. She always did. She always thought I wasn't forgiving enough of my brother and yet here I was offering the ultimate forgiveness. Again, doing what Mother wanted, but this time it felt right.

As I leave the cemetery I decide to walk instead of taking the bus. It is such a lovely day and definitely worth slowing down for. The leaves on the trees are changing colour and splashes of red, orange and bright yellow shine through the dull brown. Leaves lie in wait on the ground ready for unsuspecting feet to make them go crunch. Birds sing songs to farewell the sunshine as they prepare to settle down for the winter.

As I head along the main road I pass by a café with tables and chairs placed out on the pavement to catch the sun. Couples and families huddle together sipping on lattés and bottles of Coke. I watch as the waitress brings out a tray of drinks and cakes and places them carefully on the table of a young couple who barely look up from their phones to acknowledge her. That would never have happened in my day. How have we lost the ability to exercise simple courtesy to our fellow humans? Learning your Please-and-thank-yous was as important as mathematics in my day. A man was expected to raise his hat to a lady and open doors for her. Apart from the fact that no one wears hats anymore (such a shame as there is nothing like putting on a nice felt hat to really make you feel good), in my opinion the equality between the sexes has gone too far! I have literally seen men and women collide while entering a building as the social etiquette is no longer clear. I appreciate the women's movement, and my wife was an armchair participant, but all I see is a confused generation of young people.

I decide to stop by the café and watch for a while. There is nothing like the luxury of time and once dead one seems to have a lot of it. So I go from table to table observing every minute detail that would not have been possible when alive. The thing that strikes me is that everyone is on their phones. When I was younger phones were for calling people. Nowadays they seem to do everything but the laundry! I can see how society got to this point, but I can't see how we can get away from it. Not one single person at this café is engaging with anyone else. They all have their phones up and their heads down and if they are not tapping away at the screen, they are so engrossed in what is on it that their minds and bodies have completely lost touch with each other. They have lost their wholeness and placed it in the safekeeping of a tiny piece of metal and plastic.

I watch as person after person picks up their drink and takes a sip without taking their eyes off the screen. Their bodies may be present but their minds are elsewhere. What is the point I will never know. What is so important on that tiny screen of theirs to take away from a moment of pure enjoyment surrounded by family or friends? That first sip of a deliciously anticipated coffee while sitting in the sun, feeling the smooth liquid slide down your throat and warm you from the inside while the sun's rays warm your skin. It's one of life's little pleasures that seems to have skipped a whole generation. These days I suppose everybody wants everything now. Instant Gratification they call it, and I don't see how it is doing any good.

One small boy screams suddenly as his mother tries to wrestle the phone from him. 'Me, phone, me, phone!' he screams as his mother nervously tries to calm him by explaining that they need to go now, and he can have the phone later. As his screams move down his legs, they slide him onto the ground, his face turns red, he takes in a deep breath and... silence. Silence before the storm I suspect, and just as I think this an enormous wailing escapes the boy's mouth, so loud that it stops the workers on the building site opposite. As a few tut-tuts and disapproving stares are thrown the mother's way, she quickly pulls her phone out of her bag and hastily gives it to the boy. It's a miracle. All screaming stops, tears are quickly brushed aside, and the little body stops trembling. He scrambles to his feet, grabs the phone and happily walks away, eyes glued to the screen and oblivious to what is going on around him. What a wasted opportunity to teach one of life's important lessons! I don't really blame the mother as everyone is quick to judge these days, but I must say I feel she is making a rod for her own back. Imagine when he's a teenager!

I do worry about the children. They are no longer taught the art of conversation. One reads a lot about cyber bullying these days, and it is a terrible thing, but how can a generation of teachers and parents who have lost their own ability to truly connect with others teach the children to be any other way? The headlines in the newspapers scream about plummeting self-esteem and fast-rising rates of suicide in youth today, and at the same time talk about how loneliness is killing the elderly. We know what is going on but don't seem to be prepared to do anything! If I were Prime Minister, I would insist on mobile-free days, just as they do with occasionally limiting traffic going in and out of the city. We seem to care more for the environment than we do for ourselves and our families and that is saying something!

I walk off, having seen enough, and continue down the road. I pass by the local supermarket where we used to go to buy our milk and I see the owner putting up a Christmas display in the window. Christmas and it's only October! Honestly, I sometimes think consumerism has made us all go a bit mad! He whistles to himself as he puts up the fairy lights and smiles at his statue of Father Christmas as he lovingly places him centre stage. No Baby Jesus in sight mind you, but I suppose Jesus doesn't sell as well as Santa.

I smile as a memory I haven't accessed in years comes to mind. Our daughter was only tiny at the time and we were putting up our Christmas decorations, a tradition that we always completed on the fifteenth of December. Why? Well, it wasn't too close to Christmas Day to not be able to enjoy the decorations for a while, but it wasn't too far away either as then I felt Christmas seemed to lose its impact. Carols were playing on our tape deck and my wife had made everyone hot chocolate. We had a rather large Nativity scene at the time, which we had set up in the corner of the lounge room. Of course, the Baby Jesus wasn't in his crib yet as he technically hadn't been born, but my daughter found him in the storage box still wrapped in paper. She pulled him out of the box quietly, no-one noticing, and took him off to her room. She dressed him up in a miniature pink doll's dress she had taken from another toy and placed him lovingly in her tiny bassinet usually reserved for her favourite doll.

When Christmas Day came, we couldn't find the Baby Jesus! We searched high and low but he was no-where to be found. It wasn't until that afternoon as we all piled into the car ready to drive to my wife's sister's place for an afternoon of eggnog and more present opening, that we noticed Alice clutching a doll very tightly in her tiny arms. My wife asked to see the doll and Alice produced a firm, and very two-year-old 'NO!' 'Please darling, I just want to have a look,' pleaded my wife to which Alice replied 'No! My dolly. No show you. Me no share!' My wife realised at that point what had happened, and we all laughed. At least the mystery of the Baby Jesus had been solved.

The smell of fresh bread grabs my nose and leads it towards a shop window.

Warm, freshly baked bread has to be one of life's smallest but greatest pleasures. We didn't eat it during the week, but it was a weekend ritual that the whole family loved. The children and I would go to the bakery, little squabbles breaking out over whose turn it was to pay the baker. Back we would go, mouths salivating with anticipation. We would come home to a table laid with homemade plum jam from the tree in our garden, and room-temperature butter served in a butter dish, and most certainly not out of the plastic container!

On would go thick lashings of jam, fingers sticky and mouths grinning with pleasure. It was one of the only moments I would allow myself to let go and just indulge without consequence. My wife is an excellent baker and could have easily made the bread herself, but the trip to the bakery was part of our family ritual, and rituals are so important. They are the foundation for childhood memories in my opinion, and part of how we define ourselves.

But bread makes me think of my ducks and so I turn in the direction of the park.

CHAPTER 5

The Ducks

I WALK UP the road and through the old gate that takes me into the park. The shining sun has attracted many families and children run around shouting with glee. I walk down the slope towards the pond, past benches of parents with heads bent downwards, oblivious to the world. I continue past the ice-cream stand and the little coffee shop that hugs the far-east corner of the pond, and I take my seat.

No longer having the ability to throw out bits of bread, the ducks don't come to me, but I settle in and watch as their fog horn quacks and their grabbing beaks fight for treasure. There is a sign up near the pond asking people to offer frozen peas to the ducks instead of bread, but as I watch grandparents with grandchildren clutching the remnants of week-old bread, I realise that some traditions will never die.

One little girl nearly falls in the pond and her mother grabs the back of her coat as her toes touch the water. The father puts down his phone and jumps up calling out something in a language I don't understand, the mother nods and then he sits down on the bench again, back to his momentarily unattended business. The little girl laughs as two ducks fight over the one piece of bread, and when she turns to her mother for more, her mother shrugs and turns to walk away, the little girl not quite finished with her moment. She sits back on chubby legs, laughing and smiling at the ducks. Her mother rejoins her father and they both call out to her, ready to be on their way, the job they came to do completed. But the little girl doesn't want to leave her new friends, and she is quite content to watch their antics as they chase after the next lot of weekly scraps being catapulted at them by a five-year-old boy.

The father says something again, this time with impatient undertones, and the little girl slowly gets up, waves goodbye to her friends, and runs towards her parents full of stories about the things they have lost the ability to notice. It's at this point that I tune in to two ladies sitting on the next bench over from mine. One seems to be doing all the talking while the other sits there mumbling a few mmm hmmms from time to time. One body is agitated and leaning forwards, widely gesticulating, while the other body is protected behind crossed arms and large sunglasses.

'I just can't cope anymore,' says the first one. 'What am I, a taxi service? Just call me Mum's Taxi, available 24/7, to take you where you want to go with no thought for my needs'. She doesn't care. 'Mum, I need this, Mum I need that,' is all I hear. No 'thank you,' or no 'aren't you the best mother in the world.' I'm sick of it! My youngest is becoming even worse! She used to be the placid one, but she watches her older sister and seems to take what she learns and multiply it by ten!' She pauses for breath.

I get the feeling they don't know each very well, but I don't think the first one cares. She has found her outlet, pouring her heart and soul into it until she feels better, oblivious to the effect she is having on the other. She continues her rant about how exhausted she is, how useless her husband is and how he doesn't do anything around the house, how tiring it is to take the children from one activity to the next, to pack their schoolbags every morning, to get through the piles of unclean clothes that seem to breed overnight. The second one emits another grunt of acknowledgement, never taking her eyes off the spot in the middle of the lake where they seem to have taken refuge. The first one goes on and on about how difficult her life is, only pausing as a child in an adult's body is wheeled past by his carer. He is placed in the sun to watch the ducks and the complainer pauses for a moment while looking at him. The carer sits down on the bench next to me and lights up a cigarette.

The reverie is broken when the First One's daughter runs up to show her a pine cone she has found and the mother snaps at her 'Can't you see I'm talking!' She's then off again on her tirade about how difficult it is being her, how her children interrupt her all the time, how she never has time for herself and how no-one seems to care about her. I see the woman next to her uncomfortably shift her position, uncrossing and quickly re-crossing her arms.

I worked with someone like this once. The Energy Vampire they dubbed her in the office. Always complaining about this and that, always needing to lean on people, always upset about something. Some people are just never satisfied. They are no longer able to see the world for what it is, to give thanks for what they have and to better things when they need to. Reading the newspaper used to give me perspective. It would help me see that perhaps things in my life weren't so bad after all as I read about something awful that happened in another part of the world.

My wife, on the other hand, refused to watch the news after she watched footage of a tiny little refugee boy washed up on the shore of the land that was supposed to keep him safe. She said she couldn't cope anymore with the atrocities in the world and just wanted to focus on the happy things in her life. I didn't understand her at first, and thought she was being selfish and self-absorbed, but I realise it was a safety mechanism that she put in place to protect herself from the things she felt useless to fix. I can see that now, and I understand why she would want to do this.

I read an article recently about how world politics affects the everyday person; how the local housing market slows down as people hold on to what is familiar when faced with so much uncertainty. How workers stay in the same jobs, too afraid to let go of the security they feel they have, putting aside their aspirations for when times are better.

What if we didn't live like that? What if this 'collective consciousness' as the article called it really is a thing? I dismissed it at the time as new-age nonsense, but now as I sit here watching the sun shine down on a park full of very fortunate people, I realise that no-one appears grateful for what they have! Their children are able to run around happily and safely and in perfect health, longing for the eyes of their parents to be on them, and yet these same parents are absorbed in someone else's moment or complaining about the hardships they have to face. I feel like screaming out to them 'WAKE UP PEOPLE! You have so much good in your lives! Open your eyes and see it! Look around you! You are not running for your life or hiding your family out of fear. You are not selling your assets and handing over savings of a lifetime to an unknown person with a waterlogged boat! You are not dealing with a sick child, a dying relative or a mortgage you can't pay!' Or perhaps they are, but we only have this moment, and if we spend it thinking about the disasters of the world or the wolf at our door, we will perpetuate these situations and dig ourselves deeper into our perceived misery.

The article talked about meditation and taking time to 'just be'. About examining ourselves and our belief systems in order to figure out what is holding us back, what is getting in the way of our dreams. About forgiving past events and people, about forgiving ourselves, about creating space to allow our true selves to emerge and to shine in the sunlight. It all felt rather inwardly-focused and selfish as I read the article. Just another layer to the self-absorbed culture we are raising our children in. The 'Look at me!' culture of selfies and sharing your breakfast with the world. But I see now that I missed the point. Perhaps re-connecting with yourself and finding what truly makes you happy is the best way to heal the world.

I've never really understood art-lovers who can stare at a canvas for seemingly hours on end finding some hidden meaning in a red square on a green background. I still don't, but as I sit here in the sunshine, my memories allowing me to feel the warm rays on my skin, I look at the park in minute detail. The leaves on the trees as they start to change colour; the bright reds, the soft oranges, the dull browns. How they sway in the gentle breeze that is caressing the park, whispering to each other in a language we don't understand.

I lower my eyes and am mesmerised by the diamond-like sparkles that dance across the water. Running and leaping and chasing each other as the water moves underneath them. They hold my attention until a pebble scatters them, only to re-appear once the ripples die down.

A flock of birds suddenly take flight, flying in formation perhaps off to warmer shores as the colder weather starts to take hold. I watch as they seem to fly in perfect unison, a system of carefully devised positions allowing each bird to take a turn leading the flock, before a new one takes its place when it is time for the leader to take a break. Injured, sick or older birds have an easier time flying as they are sheltered from the head winds by their leader.

It reminds me of a documentary I once saw about African wild dogs. It talked about how they utilise their strengths and protect their weaknesses. A strict hierarchy is in place and the pack is led by the alpha pair who are in charge of the group and make decisions for them, which the rest of the group unquestioningly follow. Newborns, the injured or sick and the elderly, all very vulnerable members of the pack, are given full priority. The pups are always fed first, and no-one ever fights over food as they believe there will always be enough. Any injured or elderly members of the pack are cared for by the rest of the pack and the elderly are seen as valuable members, care and support being given to them without question.

We used to value the elderly. We used to believe that they had something to teach us, that they could lead us through our most difficult moments. But we lock them up now. We disrespect them and we believe they have nothing left to offer society. I suppose life today is so different to when they were young. Perhaps they can't teach us what we need to know as they are too disconnected from this fast-paced life we live nowadays. But perhaps that is where we can learn our biggest lesson.

Phew! I don't know if my wife would recognise this soul-searching, navel-gazing man sitting on the park bench in the midday sun! But I'm changing, I can feel it. And perhaps that is what this experience is all about.

I stand up and decide to spend time walking through the park, my park, one more time. I say goodbye to my ducks, eyes lingering just that one moment longer to watch them as they go about their daily life. I turn and commence my stroll through the nearby woodlands and to the garden of statues that has always felt to me like a magical place to be.

I've not always been a big one for modern art, having a tendency to lean towards the more classic side of life, but there is something in a sculpture, or a statue, that always captures my imagination like a painting never could. The way it looks like it could just spring to life at any moment. This creates a certain unease in me, as well as delight, depending on the type of statue or sculpture I am contemplating. This idea of a statue actually secretly being alive brings back a memory. I remember when I was a young lad and my mother took my brother and me to see a visiting circus as it passed through a neighbouring village. It was the highlight of our month, and as the days and nights slowly ticked by until circus day, I could hardly sleep with excitement!

When the big day arrived, I leapt out of bed ahead of my brother, got myself dressed, ate my breakfast and waited patiently by the front door, hair brushed to shining, boots tightly laced and polished, jacket on and buttoned up to my neck. It didn't matter that my mother and brother were still only just starting to get themselves ready, I decided to sit patiently by the front door until we were ready to leave.

When it was time to go, Mother gave a stern warning that we were both to be on our best behaviour or else we would come straight home. Not wanting to miss such an opportunity of a life-time my brother and I solemnly nodded our promise to her and we headed out the door towards the bus stop. Of course, a juvenile promise does not always last long and we were soon arguing over who was going to get on the bus first, who was going to pay the driver and who was going to sit next to Mother. We were both promptly separated, our mother sitting in between glaring furi-ously at the two of us. 'Final warning!' she said through gritted teeth, but I knew we would go no matter what; it was as much a treat for Mother as it was for us.

When we arrived at the circus, we queued up with the rest of the crowd to buy our entry tickets and then went through the gates and into another world. There were people everywhere! The crowds were huge and for a brief moment I thought I would be carried out to sea by the waves surrounding me. I gripped Moth-er's hand even tighter and leant into her side as we pushed through the crowds to go and see the World's Strongest Man who we'd seen on the posters that had been put up around our village.

We followed the crowd into the tent, a strong smell of straw filling our nostrils, and there he was, dressed in funny looking shorts, a white sleeveless T-shirt and an over-sized and very black moustache. He spoke with an accent from another land, which only added to his charm, and as he flexed his muscles and bent down to pick up a very heavy looking bell bar, I could feel his strength increasing my own until I could no longer sit still. I stood up and put my arms out next to me, bending them at the elbows to show Mother just how strong I was too! She told me to sit down and watch the show, and with a twinge of disappointment I did so, and was soon absorbed again in the incredible display before my eyes.

He juggled cannonballs, lifted a heavy bell bar with only two fingers, and held a very surprised lady from the crowd above his head. After several more displays of pure brawn we left the tent and onto the next feat of incredible talent.

We came to a tent that was different from the other ones. This one was much smaller and was covered in tiny lanterns containing flickering candles. Mother asked us both to wait outside and as she pushed back the curtain to enter, I caught a glimpse of a woman with a strange looking scarf over her head, and a table with a round clear ball on it, in front of her. The curtain closed only to quickly open again with a warning from Mother to not wander off and to wait for her there. When the curtain moved again, it was a different Mother who emerged. She looked slightly shaken and pale and she grabbed both of our hands and walked quickly away from the tent. I wondered what had happened and eventually found the courage to open my young mouth and ask if she was OK. 'It was just a silly bit of nonsense,' is all she would divulge, and I knew to let it go.

We had been asking Mother to see the mermaid that they had apparently found off the coast of Africa, or so the poster said when Mother read it to us. With excitement and anticipation, we entered the tent and there in the middle was a pool with clear sides and a beautiful iridescent green tail splashing around in it. At the other end of the tail was a beautiful mermaid, with chocolate brown skin and long flowing hair. She wore clam shells and a fishing net, which I imagined at the time was the fishing net they had caught her in, and she was simply captivating! She let out a mournful sigh, dived deep into the pool and to my utter delight swam up to my side of the pool under the water and waved directly at me! My mouth dropped open and I suddenly found I couldn't move. I was captivated and felt I had made contact with a creature from another world. I felt a hand touch my shoulder and I knew it was time to go. I waved a shy good bye and went back out into the daylight, feeling like a different person.

Our final visit was to the tent of the Human Statues and I was nervous as we followed the crowd in. It was dark inside the tent and we could make out silhouettes of people as they stood in unusual positions not moving. I was too scared to look at them directly and I allowed Mother to guide me as we walked around the room, my fingers occasionally parting before my eyes to allow a peep into the Unknown.

A bell rang, the statues changed position, and then were still again, a complete silence filling the tent. I felt my courage start to return and little by little I removed my fingers from my eyes and allowed myself to catch a nervous glimpse at what was around me. I found statue after statue up on blocks, one looking like Cupid with a bow and arrow and foot lightly held up in the air, others in positions with arms over their heads or standing on one foot, but all of them staring off in front of them, not seeing anything in the room. I felt very uncomfortable and quietly whispered to Mother that I would like to leave. This request was met with 'You're such a baby!' from my brother, but I could see the relief in his face.

So here I am, back in the garden, and surrounded by statues, but this time I know they will not come to life when a bell rings but will remain like this forever. The statues are beautiful, a dark green bronze that has dulled over time. I walk around them and take the time to contemplate each one. There is a statue of a little girl holding a cat and as I stand looking at her, a small hand reaches out in front of me to touch the statue. I turn around to see a girl of no more than three or four years old, reaching out to stroke the cat and I am struck by the incredible resemblance. Her little face stares at the statue, her eyes recognizing a four-year-old dream before her. As she runs off towards her mother, her tiny voice sweetly requesting a cat of her very own, I move onto the next statue. It is of a mother holding a baby whose little hand is reaching up to touch his mother's face. It is a beautiful moment captured by art, and as I gaze at this statue, I realise how short life really is, how quickly children grow up and how quickly we grow old. I move on to the next statue and the next, some bringing out emotions I hadn't felt in a long time. I walk past a horse, its saddle shining a bright gold in the sunshine, polished by years of tiny bottoms climbing joyously on to it. I decide to do the same and as I climb up into the saddle, I feel young again, like a little boy, the present moment full of happiness and the life ahead full of promise.

I look around the garden one more time, sadly saying goodbye but thanking it for providing me with such happy and peaceful moments over the years. I climb down off the horse and head towards the gate.

I leave the statues and continue out the other side of the woods and into an open field. A brightly-coloured diamond is flying high up in the sky. As I follow the string down, I arrive at a little boy, no more than six or maybe seven, holding on to it for dear life. I am surprised he doesn't simply take off, up into the sky to float across the rooftops of the nearby houses! But his little skinny body remains firmly on the ground, occasionally being swayed nearly off-balance by a strong gust of wind.

The kite suddenly crashes to the ground and as the little face crumples with disappointment, his father appears at his side bearing words of encouragement and support. Up goes the kite again, only to crash to the ground once more. 'Don't give up,' says the father, 'You just have to wait for the right moment and the kite will fly again.' It sounds like a metaphor for the ups and downs of life, I laugh to myself, but there is something in the connectedness between the two that holds my attention. There is another kite on the ground, still folded up, and I imagine it belongs to the father, but he is so focused on the moment with his son that it lies forgotten. The two laugh together as the kite once more takes off, and the father holds the little boy's waist for a moment while he regains his balance.

It is such a lovely moment between father and son, one of such complicity, that I stand there smiling, feeling the privilege of being witness to such a beautiful and intimate moment. The kite sways and swerves, cutting through the sky with such velocity that the father again reaches out to steady his son. 'I can do it!' says the son proudly as he sits in that delicate space between being little and being all grown-up. The kite crashes to the ground again and the father runs over to inspect the damage. 'Perhaps we should call it a day,' he says, which is instantly met with a loud protest of disappointment. 'One more try then,' the father says begrudgingly, but clearly proud that his son does not give up easily.

The diamond returns to the sky and I watch the little boy's face as he stares upwards, concentrating on control and not letting go. His little face bursts into a huge grin as the kite continues to soar, his small arms holding and controlling perfectly. His body may be on the ground, but his spirit is up there flying with the kite and I can't help but smile again as the kite makes a sharp turn and the little boy manages to keep it in the air.

'Did you see that?!' he says excitedly to his father.

'I sure did! You are doing so well! Soon I'll be able to let you fly mine.'

What a sense of achievement! I've always encouraged that in my children. It's so important to let them learn things for themselves, to let them experience the highs and lows while in the safety of a loving environment.

I leave the park, head back to the main road and continue on my walk not really knowing where to go. I turn the corner and walk past a small Italian restaurant, red and white check table cloths peering out from the window. I continue on until I come to the garage where I used to take my car when it needed more care than I could give it. I decide to go in and see if my mechanic is in today. As I enter the garage, I see legs poking out from underneath an old BMW, a foot tapping to the sound coming out of the radio. *That's him* I think to myself and I wait for the rest of his body to emerge.

When he rolls back out from underneath the car, I watch him as he tears a large piece of paper towel from a roller on the wall. He wipes the black grease from his hands and picks up a multi-meter, used for checking battery charge. He starts the car, pops open the bonnet and connects the meter to the engine. 'Come on old girl,' he says and smiles as the reading looks good. He unplugs the meter, rolling the cord back around the handset and returns it to its place on the work bench nearby. He may go home in dirty overalls but he certainly keeps a very clean garage. I always appreciated that about Chris. 'The Car Doctor' I used to call him as he could diagnose what was wrong just by listening to the engine. He knew every part of each car, inside and out, like a doctor who has studied the human body for years. Skills like his tend to go unnoticed in this world.

He washes his hands several times with industrial soap and then dries them carefully on a towel. He walks to the little office at the back of the garage, takes off his overalls and puts on a pair of clean jeans and a clean flannel shirt. He pulls on casual boots and a warm jacket, runs his fingers through his hair and turns out the light, locking the office door behind him.

He is a big man, and certainly not an elegant one, but there is a certain charm to his grizzly bear appearance. A roughness that when appreciated reflects a certain shine that you don't find with more polished people. He speaks in gruff undertones and struggles to make eye-contact when you talk to him, but I am sure that underneath that rough exterior lies a heart of gold.

As he closes and locks the large sliding door to the garage, I decide I will follow him as I haven't yet chosen who else I will visit. We cross the road, not waiting for the signal to turn green, and he waves down an approaching bus as he runs towards the bus stop.

He nods to the driver, scans his ticket and takes his seat. He stares out the window, the passing shops reflecting in his glasses.

When we arrive at his stop, he waves an appreciative thank you to the driver and steps off the bus. We walk for a few moments and turn away from the main road. After a turn into another street we walk together up to a large community hall, and I watch as Chris greets the big group of people starting to gather inside.

'Alright everybody, time to sing your hearts out!' calls a very tall, dark-skinned woman with an American accent. The group move towards the stage and start to collect together in lines.

'Right, now remember I want your bellies full of air, shoulders back and heads held high. You are singing about the Lord and I want everybody to feel the joy and hope that comes from knowing Jesus!' The small band starts up and bodies start to sway. A warmth like I have never known before comes out of open mouths and envelopes me, like a rich hot chocolate with a sprinkling of spice. They have given their attention to the choir leader but their hearts to Jesus, and the effect is mesmerising!

She stops them after a moment, asking them to return to the beginning but this time to put more soul into it. She asks Chris to step forward and he does so with a nervous cough. The choir continues until they suddenly slow down, in perfect unison and with a rich humming, allowing Chris to step into his own. He opens his mouth at the same time as his arms and liquid sunshine flows out, like a soft velvet filling the room with comfort and warmth. His voice is deep and powerful and so rich that he takes me completely by surprise. Who would have known?! The man who could barely mumble a word to his customers is now the centre of attention, singing his praises to Jesus backed up by a choir of angels! I sit down on a plastic chair and settle in for what promises to be a wonderful afternoon.

As the singing comes to a close, I watch as the choir disassembles, and people start to put their coats and hats on again. As I watch Chris walk past me, I see that he is walking taller and with a spring in his step that wasn't there before. The chatter is loud as people say their goodbyes and see-you-next-weeks and walk out of the hall and back into their everyday lives. Music has such a wonderful way of lifting people up and out of their problems. If laughter is the best medicine, then music must be the second.

I exit the hall and decide who I will visit next.

CHAPTER 6

The Goddaughter

AS I CLIMB onto the bus I notice a pregnant lady waiting her turn with a slightly anxious look on her face. She holds her work satchel protectively in front of her belly with one hand while using the other to steady herself as she starts to climb up the stairs. At the same time another passenger is trying to get on the bus and swings her elbow out in an attempt to get on first. I would like to think that she hasn't noticed that her competitor is pregnant, but either way it is a rude act of unnecessary proportions and one that makes me angry.

'Hey!' I say firmly and loudly. 'HEY!' but of course no one hears me.

Feeling disgruntled and about to launch into a mental tirade about the lack of etiquette and concern for others in today's world, I notice a woman with a toddler in a stroller and a young baby strapped to her in some sort of scarf. A teenage boy in a school uniform is standing next to her with headphones placed firmly on his ears. The woman calls out to the driver to open the back doors and I watch in amazement as the teenage boy pulls his headphones down around his neck and asks if she would like some help. With a grateful smile, and a relieved-sounding 'Yes please,' he bends down to take the front of the stroller while the mother holds on to the handles. Together they move the stroller on to the bus with a bemused toddler looking on.

Well that certainly taught me a lesson as I had completely misjudged the poor teenager. Thus, my faith is restored in humanity and the next generation.

When the bus arrives outside the school where my goddaughter works, I take my time walking up the winding path leading to the entrance. She is a high school teacher and takes great pride in transferring her love of biology to her adoring students. I feel a twinge of guilt as I have not seen her in several years and have not kept up my promise to her father, a childhood friend, that I would keep an eye on her after he passed away.

I walk along the hallway, past the rows of lockers and abandoned school bags, past the posters on the walls about student council and the upcoming sports carnival. I peep through glass-paned doors to see students looking to the front of the classroom, vague and distant stares on many faces. The bell rings suddenly and after a second's pause, doors are flung open and students pour out. The noise is like a huge explosion, and the rush of energy is incredible!

'WALK DON'T RUN!' yells a teacher, only for the words to fall on deaf ears. 'I said WALK!' Again, students continue on their own path, rudely pushing past some while smiling and laughing with others. High school was not a place I held fond memories of and I am sad to see things have not changed.

The jungle starts to go quiet as the wilderness is lured back into classrooms. As two girls walk past me I hear one ask the other what subject she has now.

'Biology,' she answers.

'Oh you're so lucky to have Jacinta,' says the other. It dawns on me then that Jacinta is Mrs Brown, my goddaughter, a certain respect for authority being lost in the familiar way today's students address their teachers.

I follow the girls until they come to a turn in the hallway and both go their separate ways.

'See you at lunch!' says the biology student, and off she goes down the hallway, leading me towards my goddaughter.

When I walk into the science laboratory I notice the chatter is still loud and unruly, but when Jacinta walks in the room, everyone immediately takes their seats, their eager faces looking up at their adored teacher. I take a seat at the back of the class and watch as the lesson starts to unfold. The passion she feels for her subject and her students is clear from the moment the lesson starts and I realise what a difference it can make to a young person's life when they are fortunate enough to have a teacher who cares. Passion is contagious and everyone has clearly caught it. I watch as Jacinta initially instructs the class and then takes her time to go around and give attention to every student.

'If you try it is this way, you should have a better view,' she says to one student, her instructions about the microscope immediately followed. 'Don't forget to note down your observations,' she says to another student. 'After all, that's what this experiment is all about!' the kind but slightly chiding tone being taken with grace.

I remember when Jacinta was a girl and how much she loathed visiting museums and anything remotely scientific. She was all about ponies and show jumping and not the least bit curious about the workings of the world in which she lived. She would shift uncomfortably whenever she was asked what she wanted to be when she grew up and would shyly answer that she just wanted to be with her beloved horses. Her parents never pushed her in any particular direction, but allowed her time to find her own feet, a gamble that has appeared to have paid off.

In her last year at school she had gone on an excursion to see an exhibition at the Natural History Museum about the anatomy of the human body, and her love for biology was born. She was not a natural student, and up until that point had floated fairly aimlessly through her studies, but there was something that she had connected with that day which had introduced her to the inquisitive and scientific mind she didn't know she possessed.

She had clearly carried this love into her working life and as I look on, I see the way her positive and enthusiastic energy passes on to each student, leaving a mark on them that they would surely carry into adulthood. Teachers play such an important role in developing and grooming our future generations, and it is wonderful when they are able to instill a love of learning in their students.

The class continues and the students remain focused. Hands occasionally rise in the air as another question is asked or another correction is sought. No question is off limits and Jacinta takes the time to give each question the focus and response it deserves.

When the bell rings, there is a slight hesitation and then each student starts to pack up. They have clearly enjoyed their class and aren't quite ready for it to be over just yet. However, as stomachs start to grumble and the promise of lunch has finally arrived, they all happily gather in a line at the front of the classroom, chatting excitedly while they keep their eyes on their teacher. I have no idea what is about to occur and so am very surprised when Jacinta moves to the door of the classroom and extends her hand to the first student in line.

'Thank you for your great work today Jonathan,' she says as she shakes the student's hand. She makes direct eye contact with him and gives him her full attention as if no-one else is in the room. The student walks out of the room smiling and the next student moves forward.

'Fantastic concentration today Emma,' and again hands exchange shakes and faces exchange smiles.

I watch as each student shakes Jacinta's hand and receives a personal comment before leaving the room and heading off to lunch. Not one compliment is the same, and each student receives the same amount of attention and positive focus, no matter who they are or where they are positioned in the line. It is only after the last student leaves that I notice Jacinta let out a large sigh as her shoulders slump slightly. She has given everything she has and it is such a gift to those students. After a moment, as she moves around the classroom packing away the last few stray items, she starts to hum, and I watch as her step lightens and her energy seems to pick up again. She may give her all to her role as a teacher but it encourages the same in return from the students and I realise too what a blessing the students are for Jacinta.

As my goddaughter walks out of the classroom and down the hall, I follow her. She pushes open a heavy door that displays a sign saying 'Staff members only' and she walks into the teachers' break room. She says hello to her fellow staff members and makes a beeline for an older-looking woman with grey hair and glasses.

'How are you Mary? Are you feeling better?' she asks.

'Oh much, thank you for asking. I used the time to recharge and am now ready to take on those little nightmares this afternoon.' Jacinta laughs and then says 'They may be nightmares sometimes, but their hearts are in the right places. I suppose they are not all geared up to be the world's next best economists but then maybe that is not what the world needs right now.'

'Humph,' grunts a fellow teacher, a man in his late forties, with a greying beard and a sour expression on his face. Without lifting his eyes off the paperwork before him he says, 'What the world needs is some smart brains to outsmart all the robots that are due to take our places very soon.'

'Now that's a sceptical comment, isn't it Richard?' asks Jacinta smiling, a concealed look of concern in her normally sparkling eyes.

'Not really,' says Richard. 'More of a realistic world view I would say. We give a good part of our lives preparing today's youth for the world of tomorrow but when the world is so rapidly changing, I am not really sure what we are preparing them for any more.' He pauses then says, 'A lot of my students don't seem so concerned about mathematics anymore, despite how I try to frame it. If I got a dollar for every time a student asked me why they need to learn maths when their phones can calculate faster than they can I'd not to be teaching for a living anymore!' He laughs at his own joke and continues marking the papers on the table in front of him.

Jacinta looks lost in thought for a moment and then says 'What the world needs perhaps, is people who are creative and right-brained. Or perhaps people who have mastered the art of being both right and left. While science and maths is extremely important, and particularly for developing a growing brain and allowing for logical thinking, I see more of the so-called soft skills playing an increasingly important role in today's society. We live in a world governed by fear, wouldn't you agree?' she asks. Richard stops marking his papers and looks up at Jacinta with a nod. He looks at her as if asking her to go on, so she continues.

'Well, fear only creates more fear and leads people to make rash and radical decisions as their egos tell them that they need to protect themselves, and it's all doom and gloom. Fear blocks thinking and blocks effective action and keeps us held in the past. Think about yourself for a moment. If you are afraid of an outcome are you going to take a step towards it? If your actions are fear-based you will be much less likely to take what your ego perceives as a risk, and much more likely to use your fear about the future outcome as the excuse your brain is looking for to not take the action.' Jacinta takes a deep breath and continues.

'Look at politics at the moment. It's a scary situation with voters being led by fear-mongers who are feeding off the negative energy that is growing every day. We are hearing about our children's future being very bleak indeed; limited jobs, the world run by machines, lack of resources and constant fighting for survival. This is all totally fear-based and not fact-based. Yes we have stuffed up the environment, and yes we need to atone for our sins. We are facing crises in the world like we have never seen before and our egos are having a field day! Our brains are wired for a negative bias and so we tend to focus on the negative in every situation instead of the positive.

'We need creative thinkers, big-picture thinkers to help move us towards a future that is positive. Sure, future generations will live a very different life to the one we live today, but it will take the creative thinkers to lead us to a better future, one where a lot of the roles we know today have been made redundant but where new ones have been created. Sure, machines have already taken over a lot of the jobs that our parents and grandparents used to do, but our children will be working in areas that are only just starting to be created now.' She takes another deep breath, pulls out a chair and sits down.

'Can't you see how important it is to fill our kids with hopes and dreams for the future?' she asks.

Richard looks at her for a moment, and then says 'OK, Jacinta, I see your point. But I would much rather be prepared for reality than for a future straight out of fairytales!' he guffaws and looks around the room for support. Mouths are silent, and eyes are now fixed on Jacinta, to see what she will say next.

She continues. 'I think that creativity is the skill of the future. While I also support maths and the sciences, I think that people who are able to tap into their intuition and instinctive insights will be much better problem solvers and therefore much better leaders. Those who are emotionally intelligent, who are aware of the emotional as well as physical needs of others, and those who are able to connect with others on a personal level, are what this world needs. And this kind of skill set can never be threatened by artificial intelligence.'

Richard remains silent so Jacinta continues. 'What about the people who are sensitive to others? What about the helpers? What about those who have the ability to connect with those around them? That is certainly something we have lost in this world and we know how much good that's done. In a world of machines we need the human touch.'

Richard thinks for a moment before starting to speak again. 'We need people who know how to create and program the machines in order to control them and keep them supporting us rather than the other way around. Machines don't need hugs, they don't need understanding, so why develop those skills? They are called soft skills for a reason!'

'Oh Richard, we have the people who are capable of what you say. We always will. But people are starting to wake up to a different way of life, a different reason for being here. Life is not, should not, be just about survival. Life is about thriving and loving and experiencing joy and remembering who we are. There is a popular school of thought that says that we are here on earth to remember what we know in the afterlife, what we knew before our birth. That we are here to awaken our consciousness and to thus create a better world. We choose our parents based on the lessons we need to learn as they are the ones who initially guide us in the world, either well through love and concern and attention, or badly through neglect, but each caregiver has been chosen with care by our souls to enable us to advance in this life, to help us learn what we need to in order to awaken and remember who we truly are.' I feel a sense of frustration in Jacinta as she pauses for a moment.

Richard jumps into the silence. 'Ok, now you've lost me. Don't turn all New Age on me. I liked you up until about three minutes ago!' Richard laughs out loud again, all the while looking slightly disturbed.

'So why do you think we are here Richard?' Jacinta asks, finally starting to lose her patience with him.

'I think we are here because of pure luck, pure coincidence. The Big Bang and all that. Come on, you're the scientist, you know this!!' Richard waves an exasperated hand in Jacinta's direction.

'What I do know Richard is that there are things we can't explain in this world. Not yet anyway, and perhaps never. But Quantum Physics is making huge advancements towards uncovering elements of life that we used to call New Age and that we will soon be able to call fact. It's all a question of energy. That is proven. Everything is energy and we have discovered that energy can be exchanged between humans, between humans and animals and even between humans and plants.'

'Plants! Jacinta, are you drunk?' he laughs again, but this time only half-heartedly. She is starting to get through to him but his belief system won't let him change his view, not yet. Jacinta smiles a tired smile and continues.

'Science proves that we are able to heal our bodies by raising our vibrational energy and by visualising the outcome. Quantum physicists are discovering more and more things that the mystics have known for centuries. Einstein was a huge advocate of imagination and the effect it has on our own life. He made many discoveries about energy and the effect it has on our environment. His work on energy transfer has been taken over by other scientists since, and we are making real headway. He strongly believed that what we imagine now creates our future. Thoughts are energy and as like attracts like, positive thoughts attract positive events, and negativity attracts only more negativity.'

'Fine,' Richard intercepts. 'But a lot of that is all talk and no action, right?! Where's the everyday proof?' he demands.

Jacinta rises to the challenge. 'A simple yet powerful example is the experiment I ran recently with my tenth graders. You would know about this if you had bothered to show up to our presentation. But anyway... I placed two plants in the classroom, both identical plants, and the same size and age. Every time my students came into the classroom they knew to speak to one with loving and kind words, to tell the plant it was loved, it was wanted, that they enjoyed having it in their classroom, and to encourage it to grow. I also taught the children how to project positive feelings on to the plant, to sit in front of it, close their eyes and think about a lovely warm and positive energy leaving their bodies and going into the plant.

'The other plant received the opposite treatment, and was told it was ugly, that it was hated, that the students wished it wasn't alive, that it wasn't wanted in the classroom. They would throw hateful and angry words at it and then walk away, not giving it any more attention.

'We also had a control plant that wasn't spoken to at all. It was watered and looked after in a completely normal way. It only had the elements needed for normal growth; light, water and shelter, but nothing else.

'And guess what happened Richard? The plant that received the positive energy far outgrew the one that was mistreated. It grew taller faster, it was healthier, it was greener than either the badly treated plant or the control plant.' Jacinta takes a breath and leans back in her chair.

'But Jacinta, again as a science teacher you know that your results are not statistically significant if you only have a few plants!' Richard exclaims.

'I know that, but this experiment was not my idea. It has been replicated on a large scale, with enough plants to make the results reliable. And the results were the same as in our classroom experiment! The transfer of energy is real, Richard! If we do this to plants with just our words and our energy, imagine what we are doing to each other! And the frustrating thing is that it is so easy to fix but no-one seems to see this yet! We reversed the experiment for the badly treated plant and started to praise it and to tell it we loved it and to project positive thoughts and energy on to it, and it started to thrive! We kept watering it at the same level, we didn't give it any extra fertiliser or a different position in the classroom with more sunlight. All we did was change the way we treated it and look what happened!

'This is real Richard, and this is the kind of world I want these kids to grow up in. A world where we realise the value of positive thoughts and gratitude and love. Not a world where we fear the future and imagine only the worst. Our thoughts create our reality, and that is not some hippy idealistic dream. Einstein knew this, but never managed to find a way to help the masses understand. But there will be others, there are already others, who know this and who are finding ways to get through to our fear-filled ego-led brains and help us see the world for what it is really is. We have created everything we see before us now, the negative is all our fault and the positive is all our own doing as well. To awaken to this realisation is what the world needs, and then we can have anything, create anything, live any life we want. And machines can still be part of that world, but if we imagine them as helping us by taking away the time-consuming and menial tasks, then we will have the time to really enjoy the life we have been given. We can spend time stopping to smell the roses and to appreciate all the good in the world, and all the good in our lives!' Jacinta barely pauses for breath before continuing.

'Here's a thought for you Richard. Perhaps this new wave of consciousness is the Second Coming. Christ lived in total connection with his fellow man and was able to guide the world and move us towards the direction we needed to go in. We are starting to see this happen again as more and more people awaken to the true meaning in life, their true purpose.'

'Whoa there, I think you're going a bit far with the Second Coming reference,' Richard says holding his hand up in the air, palm facing Jacinta. I can feel she is so close to convincing him to open his mind at least, but it is a very fine line to walk, and one that she has to tread very carefully. Jacinta's face starts to soften, and she lets out a big sigh.

'Perhaps this is too much of a subject to discuss on our lunchbreak, but all I ask of you Richard is to simply hear what I am saying and turn it over in your mind. It is OK to have a different view from each other but don't let yourself be eaten up by bitterness or fear. We all have a choice and we all create the path along which we walk so make yours a happy one. Your happiness affects the world much more than you realise.'

With that she stands up and heads towards the fridge, taking out a small plastic container. She takes a fork out of the drawer in the little kitchenette and sits back down at the large dining table to eat her lunch. The lady who had spoken earlier sits down opposite her, gives her a warm smile and briefly reaches over to squeeze her hand.

I sit down next to Jacinta and look her deep in the eyes. I tell her to never give up. That she will change the world with her passion. Never give it up. Never give up the passion that she feels for life and for those in her life. The world needs her and people like her, if a true awakening is to take place, and a positive future is to be created. We all have a choice in this life so why choose fear?

I stand up and head towards the door of the staff room. I pause to look back in the room one more time; Richard has returned to his papers but seems more pensive than before and the rest of the staff have returned to what they had been doing before the debate began. Jacinta's shoulders are slouched but she has done a good job and should be proud of herself. I am certainly proud of her. I say a silent goodbye and walk back into the hallway, along past the lockers and discarded items, and out into the daylight again, thinking about the effect one person can have on another. As I walk back down the winding path, and onto the street, my mother's carer comes to mind. Someone I hadn't thought of in a long time but someone who had really touched our lives in so many ways.

CHAPTER 7

The Nurse

IT TOOK A long time for Mother to die. I sound quite cold when I say that but I suppose having spent years living with a very practical and highly-unemotional person, I find myself responding in kind. I don't mean to, really. I loved her very much and tried to be close to her but she was from another generation, a wartime generation whose forte was survival and rations and the re-use of teabags.

Mother had been ill for quite some time but not being one to make a fuss, we hadn't known. We had noticed what appeared to be dementia slowly creeping in, but then Mother was in her eighties, so it wasn't really surprising. It was during her weekly shopping trip, when I would accompany her, that I noticed her hand shake as she tried to place a loaf of bread in the shopping trolley. I asked her if she was feeling OK, and she smiled a wan smile and told me the truth. She was dying. Right there in the supermarket. Just like that. Well, she wasn't dying in the supermarket, but she told me that her doctor had given her six months at the most, and that she didn't want me making a fuss about it. She had already spoken to her solicitor and had the will and her personal property sorted out and 'Could you be a dear and organise a nurse to visit me at home when I need it?' She continued on her way down the aisle leaving me standing there staring like a stunned rabbit in the headlights.

We didn't say much as I helped her into the car and placed the groceries on the back seat. We still didn't really talk as I drove her home and helped her out of the car and in through the front door. I put the kettle on and made us a cup of tea and it was then that she opened up. She had cancer, and while she was feeling alright at the moment, the doctor had said it was widespread and she wouldn't live to see next Christmas. She took a sip of tea and I half expected her to talk about the weather. That was Mother. Never a more practical woman did I ever come across.

When she finished her tea, I took our cups to the sink and rinsed them with hot water, not really noticing as I burned my hands under the tap. My mind was racing and my words had gone into hiding. She had been very clear about not wanting to go in to a home or hostel and wanting to live out her days in her own house. That I could understand.

I found an agency that manages home care for the elderly and they sent us a nurse called Ann. When my wife and I opened the front door to her on her first day, she greeted us with a firm handshake and then went over to Mother, sat down next to her and explained who she was and how she saw their relationship working. She explained that she was there to help Mother around the house, to help her get dressed and to enable her to live the most normal life possible. She would be able to take her shopping and to medical appointments and could administer any medication as necessary. Due to Mother's advanced age and condition, her goal was to make Mother's last days on earth as comfortable and easy as possible.

I felt very reassured from the moment I laid eyes on Ann. I could tell she would take no nonsense from Mother but would also be the loving and kind bringer of dignity that everyone deserves when their life on this earth is drawing to a close. We decided to give Mother some time alone with Ann to ensure that they would be able to get on and that Mother would be comfortable with her and happy with our choice. We agreed we would come back later that day to see how she was settling in.

It can't have been easy looking after someone you don't really know, but Ann took on her role with grace and dignity. She was a fine nurse, medically speaking, which Mother needed, but she was able to take care of the emotional side of things too. Mother had a lot of medication to manage and we were very grateful that Ann could be there to help her.

As the weeks went on, everything seemed to be running smoothly. Ann and Mother had a good relationship and I could see that Mother was being very well taken care of. But it was on one of my regular visits, as I was climbing out of the car outside the house, that I heard an angry voice jumping out Mother's front window and down the street.

'Thief!' I heard her yell as I walked through the door. 'Get out of my house! THIEF!' I rushed into the house to find Mother red-faced, leaning forward in her lounge chair and waving an angry fist at poor Ann.

'Oh thank goodness you're here,' Mother said. 'She stole my pearl necklace!' The woman who cared deeply for my mother and took care of her every need had now been reduced to 'she.'

'I am sure there must be some reasonable explanation,' I said, as I walked over to Mother's side with a glass of water in hand to try to help her calm down.

'NO!' she screeched. 'She is a thief and I want her out of my house!' screamed Mother, determination, anger and a feeling of injustice pouring out of every pore.

I took Mother into her room to have a lie down, promising that I would look for her necklace while she rested. As I started to look I began to wonder what could have happened to the necklace. Had Ann really taken it? We weren't able to pay her much and so maybe she needed to top up her weekly earnings, and I'm sure the necklace could have been sold for a reasonable amount. I started to feel very guilty and worried about leaving Mother with a complete stranger, particularly when she was in such a vulnerable state. Ann had come with good references from a good agency, but you never really know someone. I had been so relieved to be able to leave Mother in what I thought were very capable hands, that I had happily signed the contract and handed the care of my elderly mother over to a middle-aged and possibly dishonest stranger.

Ann looked very embarrassed and rather horrified and explained that she had no idea where the necklace could be. She said Mother had been very forgetful lately and that perhaps she had misplaced it somewhere. We both kept thoroughly searching and after about ten long minutes, Ann held up a triumphant hand clutching a string of pearls.

'I found them!' she beamed, relief written all over her face. She had discovered them in the cutlery draw next to a misplaced tea bag. The guilt I had felt just moments earlier about Mother quickly turned into guilt about Ann. I had completely misjudged her in the heat of the moment. I mumbled my apologies and thanked her for finding the necklace. I went to tell Mother the good news but found her sleeping so I agreed with Ann that I would come back later that day.

When I came back in the afternoon Ann called out to me from the bathroom. I walked in to find Mother leaning back in a chair, head held backwards over the sink, a large towel placed on the floor and a bucket of warm water placed on the towel. Ann was washing my mother's hair with the care a mother takes of a newborn. Using a plastic jug to tip water from the bucket over Mother's hair, with each rinse she would gently run her empty hand from Mother's forehead down through her hair to stop the water from falling in her eyes. Mother's face looked so relaxed and calm, nothing like it had been a few hours earlier. 'She' had become 'Ann' again in mother's eyes, and the difference was startling. I stood there dumbfounded by how Ann had been able to transition from a hated enemy to a loving carer again in a matter of hours. How Ann could care for someone so difficult in such a loving way astounded me.

I was struck by the fact that we are all quick to judge others without really knowing them or the circumstances that surround them. There is constant talk in this world about the negative side of human nature and yet standing here before me was the perfect reminder of how incredible people really can be. For every dreadful act in this world there is always an equally kind and loving act, but it is these acts that quite often go unnoticed.

As Mother's health worsened, so did her dementia. Ann would sit for hours with Mother, on her lucid days playing cards, and on the days when Mother couldn't remember what the symbols on the cards stood for, Ann would read to her. She would cook and clean for her, do her laundry and take her out for walks to the park to sit and watch as life went by. It really is amazing how someone who is effectively a stranger can come into someone else's life and take care of them like they are their own family. We were all truly blessed by Ann's presence.

Mother made it to Christmas, stubbornly defying the doctor's prediction. It was an emotional Christmas and one that we all wanted to remember. After plates were scraped clean, Christmas crackers were picked up, eager hands pulling on each end. Out fell the bad jokes and the equally bad paper hats but everyone wore them with pride that day, including Mother. After Christmas pudding was consumed, the children went to their rooms to listen to the CDs they had received for Christmas, Mother went to have a lie down and my wife and I moved into the lounge room with her brother, Alan, to relax and reminisce in front of the fire.

As the brandy was poured the stories started to flow and I was reminded of the period when my wife and I had moved in with my parents as newlyweds as we were trying to save for a house. My wife told us the story of the first time she used my parents' very old-fashioned shower – the type where you had to light a match in the gas box to light the flame that would heat the water. It was in the days of bouffant hairstyles and lots of hairspray and as my wife leaned her head backwards away from the water so as not to get it wet, her nose started to twitch, and a burning smell started filling the bathroom. She suddenly realised her hair was on fire! She let out a blood curdling scream and Mother came running into the bathroom to see what had happened. When she caught sight of my wife and her blazing hair, she immediately threw water over it from the shower, and then stated sternly: 'What a fuss you are making! I thought something serious had happened!'

And with that she left the bathroom, my poor wife standing there, hair dripping, not knowing how to react. We all laughed at that memory, a different perspective and a certain fondness that usually installs itself with time and distance.

I remembered how it was always Mother who we would ask to remove unwanted spiders from our bedrooms, or to fix our toys when they were broken. She used to buy chickens from the butcher still wearing their coat of feathers, and she would pluck them herself, a bowl in her lap to catch the feathers as she sat on the back doorstep facing out to the garden.

I remembered the old apron she wore for most of my childhood, always patching it up as necessary, and the countless costumes she would make us for our school plays. I thought about the gentle kiss she would place on our foreheads as she tucked us in to bed and bent over to say goodnight, the only dose of affection we would receive from her.

'She's a tough old thing,' Alan said into his brandy glass. 'You'd have to soak her overnight to kill her with an axe.' My wife and I burst out laughing, used to Alan's often morbid and very dry sense of humour.

Mother rapidly deteriorated after Christmas and on a cold February day, as snow was falling outside the window, her spirit left this world. By a miracle, the whole family was with her. Ann had called us that morning and said that Mother was not very coherent and that from her experience didn't have long to live.

She suggested we come and spend time with her and just be with her so that she could feel our presence even if she was not able to communicate with us.

We had all gathered around her bed and were telling her stories about our daily lives, lives that she had not been able to be part of for the last few weeks due to her worsening condition. I was holding her hand as my wife was telling her about the neighbours across the street and the loud car that their teenage son had recently bought, when Mother took a strange rattling breath and then her hand went limp. My wife stopped talking and I looked up at Ann, who had been quietly standing in the corner of the room. She came over to Mother, placed her hand on her frail wrist and looked off into the distance for a brief moment.

'She's gone,' she said quietly. 'I am so sorry,' she said. 'I'll let you say your goodbyes.' I heard my wife sob and my children started to cry. I could only stare at the woman who had given birth to me, scolded me, brushed my grazed knees to get the dirt off when I fell over as a little boy, fed me, and taught me to be brave. And now she was gone. I felt empty. I sat there not knowing what to do or how to react. I held on to her hand, not wanting to let her go, knowing that it was already too late. My wife took the children out of the room to give me a moment alone, and I sat there not moving. She looked so at peace after all these months of pain and illness, memory loss and loss of dignity. Now she was with her beloved angels and I knew that she was safe.

I picked up her hand and gave it a kiss. I then leant over her and delicately brushed her hair back from her face with my hand, something I never would have been able to do when she was alive. I leant down and kissed her gently on the forehead. 'Goodbye Mother,' I whispered. 'I love you.' I left the room in search of consolation from my family. Then I had to be strong and help the children through losing their grandmother.

We invited Ann to the funeral which she accepted with grace. She chose to sit in the back of the small church, not allowing herself to be part of the family despite having been closer to Mother in her final days than anyone. When the funeral was over, and I was saying my thank yous and goodbyes to the family and friends who had attended, I noticed Ann standing discreetly to the side of the church door. I put my hand in my pocket and felt for a soft piece of cloth I had placed there earlier. I walked over to Ann and thanked her for being there today as she had been there for Mother throughout her ordeal. I thanked her for making Mother's last days on earth some of the happiest of her life and for helping us as a family to get through the slow and painful demise of a matriarch. I put my hand in my pocket and pulled out the piece of cloth.

'I have something for you that I believe you deserve,' I said. I handed her the cloth and as she took it, it fell open and there was the pearl necklace. She looked down at it, looked up again and opened her mouth to protest.

'No, I insist,' I said. 'And I know if Mother were here now, she would agree.' With that I closed her hand over the small package and she smiled at me. A gentle smile, one filled with a mix of emotions. A smile full of gratitude for the gift and for the shared joke at the circumstances surrounding the necklace, but also of sadness as she had truly grown fond of Mother and had enjoyed her time with her overall. Ann was a giver and always would be, there for others at the expense of herself. It is nice to give back when one can. Givers are the salt of the earth and we need to take care of them and show them our appreciation whenever we can.

She walked out of the church and out of our lives, on to the next family who needed her to carry their loved one over into the next world with the love and kindness she had shown Mother. As I turned back to the church and the remaining family, I thanked God for Ann and the presence she had been in our lives.

As I think of my family once again, my daughter comes to mind and I know there are some little people I would like to spend time with before I have to say goodbye.

CHAPTER 8

The Daughter

I AM LOOKING forward to visiting my daughter and my grandchildren, and I feel that familiar sense of happy anticipation begin to rise as I head up their street. The house appears on the left and I see the little tricycle we gave the youngest for Christmas last year sitting in the front garden. Abandoned next to the tricycle on the grass is Teddy, which they will be frantically looking for at bedtime. Little Oliver is in the bad habit of leaving Teddy wherever he goes and forgetting about him. I suppose it is his clever two-year old way of delaying bedtime as the Hunt For Teddy begins every night at 7.15pm. Bath is done, dinner is eaten but where is Teddy? Oliver can't possibly go to bed without Teddy! 'Teddy, Teddy!' the children call, laughing as they look under couches and inside cupboards. The parents look on highly unamused, but that's part of the game when you are two.

I walk through the house and hear voices coming from the back garden. I walk through the sliding doors and out on to the terrace, and there is little Oliver sitting with my daughter intently playing with Play-Doh. I watch as his chubby little dimpled fingers press into the Play-Doh trying to shape it into something he is not yet capable of making. I admire the look of determination on his face while his eyes sparkle with pure two-year old joy. Anything is possible to him. He has not yet learned the grown-up talent of disbelief. Of talking ourselves out of things. Of telling ourselves we are not capable.

There were many times I told my daughter that she couldn't do or be something. I was trying to protect her from disappointment, and to prepare her for reality, but actually I was killing off her spirit of curiosity. I was moulding her to life as it currently was rather than teaching her to mould life to what she wanted it to be.

I watch as she encourages Oliver to not give up as signs of frustration start to show. The Play-Doh isn't doing his bidding and with a grunt of frustration I watch as he throws it to the floor, saying 'Naughty Play-Doh, bad Play-Doh,' and crossing his little arms firmly over his body. My daughter gently picks it up and encourages him to try to make something different, but he has had enough and he turns and flees toward the safety of his firetruck. That is something he can control.

I hear squeals of laughter as my granddaughter comes hurtling around the corner of the garden being chased by her father. He catches her and throws her high in the air, both laughing as she lands in his arms and they tumble to the ground together. I am amazed at what a different relationship my daughter has with her husband versus the one I had with my wife. In my day, men were expected to be the breadwinners while the women looked after the children and the household. Never would a man think to take time off to care for the children, but this is exactly what happened after our granddaughter was born.

Alice had suffered from terrible postnatal depression. She had been a high-flying executive when she met her husband. They had both travelled the world for their respective jobs and both were very happy with the arrangement. Then marriage came and the inevitable desire to start a family. She worked right up to the birth, never letting up despite the exhaustion she felt. There were a few scares along the way, but she has always been a stubborn little thing, and despite warnings from the doctor to slow down, she kept up the pace as best she could and gave birth one week early to our beautiful granddaughter.

But things didn't go as planned. The baby cried a lot and Alice found she was not able to switch off and was barely sleeping. She felt under pressure to be the perfect mother, to get back into shape and to keep living life at the pace to which she had been accustomed before the pregnancy.

She came to our house one day in floods of tears saying that the baby wasn't feeding properly and that she didn't know what to do. She looked utterly exhausted and miserable, and I didn't know what to do for her. I left her with my wife as I believed it was women's business and I went out for a walk. I felt useless and lost and desperately wanted to help my baby girl but didn't know how. I never really accepted her growing up. She was always my little girl and someone I felt compelled to protect, and I didn't know how to relate to her as an adult. I felt we lost some of the closeness we had had when she was a child as I wasn't able to adjust to her leaving childhood. I struggled with the idea of her dating boys and becoming a wife and someone else's sweetheart.

The day she announced she was pregnant was a strange one for me. It clearly marked the end of her childhood in my eyes, despite the fact she was thirty-five, and while I was excited at the idea of becoming a grandfather, I felt the ground move out from underneath me that day.

When I first held my tiny granddaughter in my arms I cried. I quickly wiped away the tears as I didn't want anyone to see, but I felt this intense connection to her, and felt those same feelings I had felt when I had first held Alice as a newborn baby.

When Alice was born, I had not been allowed in the birthing room. I waited anxiously with the rest of the new dads in the waiting room, nervously pacing as we heard the next round of screams and grunts. As the nurse would bring a tightly wrapped bundle to the waiting room window, all heads would snap up wondering if this was ours, and then most heads would bow again, staring at empty palms.

Alice didn't cry when she was born, the nurse said. She had turned blue and had to be taken away for resuscitation. She sure made up for it in those first few days of life, but what a way to start! The nurse finally brought a tiny pink bundle to the waiting room, asked for Mr Jones and angled the bundle down towards me so I could catch the first glimpse of my daughter. As the nurse left with the baby, the other men in the room shook my hand and patted me on the back with mumbles of congratulations, each of us looking just as lost and proud and choked up on emotion as the next. I sat back down and waited until the nurse came to tell me that I could see my wife.

Babies weren't given straight to the mother in those days, and while I see the benefits of the way it is done today, when I think about what my daughter went through when she became a mother, I do question whether we have gone too much the other way. My wife remained in the hospital for another three days while the nurses took care of Alice, even encouraging her to go out to dinner with me on the last night before she went home. There wasn't that expectation for an immediate bond with the baby that Alice found so hard when it was her time to become a mother.

When a child is born, a parent is born, and the transition from corporate high-flyer to mother was a hard one for Alice. She accepted this and was able to reach out for help, and luckily for her was able to get through it. But it opened my eyes to things I took for granted with my own wife. I noticed how much more involved Alice's husband was with the kids, and as I stand here watching him now, I feel a wave of gratitude for how things have changed.

I look over at my granddaughter in her princess dress and tiara and wonder what she will do with her life. The world is truly her oyster, as they say, but I worry about all the choices that stand before her. The world is changing so rapidly now, and there is all this talk about machines taking the place of flesh and blood. What if the path she chooses to take is not always available to her? I suppose a certain amount of adaptability is being taught these days and people don't seem quite as concerned with change as we used to be. There are systems in place now to help companies transition from one state of being to another, as their old identity no longer conforms to the new way of the world.

But I digress again. I want to soak up this moment with my family. Just truly enjoy being with them as they live their lives, the little ones absorbed in the moment, as we all should try to be. I love how children play. They don't question themselves or what makes sense. They just lose themselves in the very act of creation, inhibitions not yet learned, and hearts not yet broken. Dreams and reality are blurred at this age and that is where the best moments of imagination are born.

I watch my granddaughter playing in the sand, watching her on the cusp of becoming a big girl, while still wanting to remain little. She always looked much smaller when tucked up in bed at night. Her six-year-old attitude was firmly packed away as she cuddled up to her blankie, reminding me to leave her night light on so Mummy and Daddy could come and give her a kiss goodnight when they came back from dinner.

She had been having a hard time lately as she discovered for the first time just how mean kids at school could be. She is a very loving and caring child and would get very upset if anyone called her names or accidently pushed past her while rushing into school when the bell rang. She could never understand why kids wouldn't apologise when they had hurt somebody, even if by accident, and she really felt the injustices of the world.

She is a perfectionist and the teacher was getting frustrated with her at school. One day over Sunday lunch Alice recounted how the teacher had really put my granddaughter down in front of her classmates when she coloured an autumn leaf blue rather than the usual red, orange or yellow. What we took for creativity the teacher took for non-conformity and that certainly wasn't allowed. My daughter told how she came home from school, shoulders slumped and an air of complete defeat around her. She believed herself to be 'not very good' and she said the teacher didn't like her. Well that sent my daughter into a tailspin, as she spouted words about crushing her spirit and the like.

While I can see where my daughter was coming from, I must admit that it is hard on teachers these days. The classroom sizes are much bigger than they used to be, and I wonder what the effect of them losing some of their authority has had. While I don't agree with corporal punishment, as used to be the norm when I went to school, I still believe there needs to be a certain amount of respect, and I don't see this anymore. Teachers are called by their first names and the children know that they don't wield much power. It must be a tough role to play, but it is also an incredible opportunity to be able to shape such small minds and to instill a love of learning and an encouragement of curiosity into their hearts.

As a parent I know how tiring small children can be, and how much easier it is if everyone simply does as you ask. But it is a shame when a teacher lets an opportunity for encouraging individualism, self-belief and imagination be lost, and so I can understand why my daughter was upset. There is so much pressure on everyone these days; pressure to perform, to get good grades, to be above-average. Individualism gets lost in the need for comparison and comparison is the effect of conformity.

I pushed both my children to go to university and now I wonder whether I did the right thing. Why do we have to fit a mould? What would happen to humanity if more of us were allowed to follow our dreams? When we view life as having finite resources, we create an unhealthy and unnecessary competition. If we believe there are not enough jobs to go around, not enough money, not enough food we see the next person as competition, as someone we must be better than. We push our children in a direction they perhaps don't want to go in out of fear. We call it love but really it is our fear of the unknown that we project on to them.

I remember my son coming home one day having won an award for his clay sculpture he had entered in a school art competition. He glowed with pride and possibility and announced, at the ripe old age of fourteen, that he had found his calling. Well, I suppose he didn't quite say it like that but that is what I heard. And I panicked. I suddenly saw dreams being washed away as I imagined my son working as a starving artist, struggling to make ends meet as he tried to carve a living from a passion. I didn't believe it was possible to combine the two, which I suppose looking back now was quite naïve. Out of what I believed to be concern and love for him, I insisted he give up his art studies when the time came to choose the subjects for the following year, and I worked through the pangs of guilt by telling myself that I was not crushing a dream but that I was the parent and I had the experience to know what was best for my own child.

My wife didn't agree with me at the time, but I would not budge. No son of mine was going to be a sculptor when there would be bills to pay and responsibilities to assume. But what if parents have got it wrong and children have it right? Are adults too blinded by their fears and personal experiences to see what really matters? Is it fair that subdued or shattered dreams come to life again through our children? Children are born with an innate ability to connect to life at a different level, and through practicality and what adults call reality, we slowly disconnect them from this to ensure they conform with life as we know it, as we experience it. But what if we let ourselves be led by their childish simplicity, what if we encouraged their dreams rather than suppressed them? There are many paths a child could follow but not all lead to happiness. We need to support our children while they are young, and create healthy and well-balanced children rather than spend our time fixing broken adults. We throw around words about living the life of our dreams, but we are too afraid to really do it. But what if we followed the lead of our children?

There is a lot of stress involved with being a parent these days. Not that it was easy when my children were young, but there are so many choices, too many choices, and that is a natural creator of stress. However, I feel the balance is perhaps better for my daughter today than it was for my wife. There are options today that didn't exist when we were young parents. And as I watch my little granddaughter being chased by her father through the garden, I realise how involved young fathers are these days. Times are changing, and we need to accept that and work with it, but people are not always good with change.

I sit down on the terrace and watch my family. I soak up the joy in my young grandchildren's faces, such simple but all-encompassing and powerful joy. They are lost in the moment, completely unaware of anything but this moment they are living.

Little Oliver spots a butterfly and on wobbly legs he starts to chase it. He falls down but never takes his eyes off the butterfly, and as he scrambles to his feet again the butterfly takes flight in search of its next flower. Oliver is fascinated. 'Flutterby, Mummy, Flutterby,' he squeals, and I realise just how much our children have to teach us. The joy to be found in the simplest of life's pleasures. The putting aside of worldly worries and just being. Allowing the energy of life to move us along and to carry us when needed, not being weighed down by negative thoughts and stress.

Is worrying a habit we pick up from our parents, or is it something we are born with? Is it a learned behaviour or are our brains simply wired that way? I never believed in sheltering my children from the world, thinking instead that discussing world events at the dinner table was a way to prepare them for life on their own later on. But I think a certain innocence should be maintained, and in fact encouraged. The world changes so rapidly, but our views and opinions stay the same. What will change that? A new perspective is needed, a new way of living and what if the clue was in front of us all this time? What if our children could guide us, before they lose their innocence? Tiny souls still connected to another world, not yet tainted by this one. The joy of discovery, the joy of connection, the joy of unconditional love before the world adds conditions.

I sit here for a moment longer just watching. I have loved spending time with my grandchildren, in a way that was not the same with my own children. Maybe I didn't have to worry so much about their education and could just enjoy being with them. I really came into my own as a grandfather. I gave myself permission to play and laugh and be with them. Their little soggy kisses on my cheek as they sat cuddled up in my lap. Their weeny soft hands inside my big rough one. Their tiny fingers wrapped around my thumb as they fell asleep in my arms. They adored me and I adored them. They called me Pop and I loved it. I loved them. I still do.

I stand up rather begrudgingly, but I know I must move on. I say to the little family I see before me to always look after each other, to always laugh together and create joy together. To always be there for each other and to be each other's solace, a safe place to return to after a tough day out in the world.

I reach out and place my palm against my daughter's cheek. 'Take care my angel. You have been such a good daughter to me. You have always shown me love and care and concern. You have never judged me. You may have disagreed with some of the decisions I made over the years, but I think you see now that I made those decisions with your best interests at heart. You see that now that you are a parent. I will miss you. I am so proud of you, for your strength, your courage, your resolve. Please take good care of your mother. She will need you now more than ever.' I gently pull my hand back, take a deep breath and take one more moment to soak in the happy domestic scene before me. It is time to leave. I have another grandchild to visit.

CHAPTER 9

The Son

AS I WALK up to my son's house I can hear music coming from the upstairs bedroom. Complicated and intricate notes float down from the open window calling me to them. I follow them inside, up the stairs and into the bedroom of my teenage grandson. I sit down quietly in the corner of the room and just watch. I suppose I should say listen rather than watch, but there is something so mesmerising in the way my grandson holds the violin and sways his body as he plays. His fingers move and vibrate and control and command, but it is his body that leads the way. His body is playing the music, not just his hands. When I watch my grandson play I understand the expression to 'put your heart and soul' into something. The music and he are one. The violin is an extension of him, a tool, a way for his soul to shine through and connect with the world. He is transformed in this moment, and his transformation reaches out and transforms others. Music is contagious, it reaches out and captures the audience, pulling them in, demanding something of them. A piece of their soul perhaps? Or is it the other way around? The music adds to our soul?

I'm getting all philosophical again, but I wonder now why I didn't let myself be like this when I was alive? To get lost in something other than reality. To let myself float away from time to time, to be carried into another layer of reality that we are too busy to normally see.

I never played the violin myself, but I can appreciate the hours of practice per day that it takes to be as good as my grandson. The discipline required, the shoulder and finger cramps he used to complain about, the missing out on normal teenage life because of a need to practice, the additional stress of music exams on top of the exams he had to sit for school. I really admire my grandson for that. I never had that strength and while I took comfort in the repetition of daily tasks, as they provided me with a routine, it had nothing to do with bettering myself, or perfecting a skill, that kept me locked in a repetitive pattern.

Justin must have received some comfort or enjoyment from the daily practicing of scales and the playing of complicated pieces written by even more complicated minds. We only do the things that bring us rewards in life. But I think from a young age he was able to tap into a knowledge that seems to have escaped most people; the fact that we all must have long-term goals to strive for if we are not to give up. It's all about instant gratification these days, and the idea of striving for a goal that may be years off in the future is inconceivable to a large number of the population. The internet has brought that about. I think the more modern style of parenting hasn't helped either.

One thing I will say about my son and his parenting style was that he never gave in to Justin's demands for things. Never gave in to toddler tantrums in the supermarket because Justin had spotted a toy he wanted and he wanted it now! Benjamin would always acknowledge Justin's desire, but would not give in to his immediate need. Depending on which was closer, Christmas or his birthday, he would tell Justin that he would put the item on the present list and that Justin would receive it then. Of course, this usually wasn't the case as Justin would have moved on to another item that he wanted, and the previous item would be forgotten, but he was able to teach Justin that it is OK to want things, but that we can't always have everything we want straight away. He also ensured that Justin felt listened to, and understood, as he would acknowledge Justin's feelings and interests instead of pushing them away or ignoring them.

As I look at Justin now, I see that this has paid off. Justin understands the need to strive for something in the future, to look forward to it, and that just because he can't have it now doesn't mean he can't have it. It's not just about work ethic and understanding the rewards of hard work, but more about the fact that we can all have anything we want in life, but some things take longer to come to us than others, and that is OK.

The lesson I have learned from my teenage grandson is that without a goal it is too easy to give up. When things get tough, or you don't feel like putting in the work needed to achieve your goal, without a big picture or even a role model to look up to, it is too easy to throw in the towel and walk away.

Justin went through a few moments like that throughout the years, but he would put on a CD of his favourite violinist, or watch a DVD of him in concert, and his desire would be restored again, the knowledge that if his favourite hero could do it, he could do it too.

I remember taking Justin to see his hero live when he was performing with the London Symphony Orchestra. We both donned a jacket and tie and caught the train into London. Justin was only twelve years old, and I felt so proud as I thought about his peers most likely at home playing video games while Justin was off to enjoy a life-altering cultural experience. Not that there's anything wrong with video games, but the maturity and perseverance that Justin showed was truly commendable.

I see three reasons for someone being able to pursue a goal and not letting that little voice in their heads stop them from succeeding; firstly, they believe in themselves and their ability to achieve the goal. Secondly, the goal has a proper role to play in their life. For Justin, I knew that he wanted to be First Violinist of a world-famous orchestra, and that goal kept him going. Thirdly, one must derive a sense of pleasure or a sense of satisfaction from the goal and the work needed to achieve the goal. Otherwise one simply wouldn't pursue the goal (of their own volition that is).

Justin told me on that trip into London that when he plays the violin he goes into a trance and he feels like he has been transported somewhere else. He is taken away from his daily worries, and he is filled with joy. He is right in the moment, and he can only feel happiness there, and no negative emotions, in his meditative state. He came to me a few months after the concert we shared together, as he was upset and needed someone to talk to. He said he had tried to talk to his father, to explain how he feels when he plays, but that my son just could not understand what was so important to Justin. His response was that Justin needed to focus on something more serious and that he didn't want him to be another struggling musician, who couldn't pay the bills and was waiting tables just to survive. I know that Benjamin said this to Justin out of love and concern for him, but Justin never managed to see it that way and he said to me that he didn't know what he would do if he couldn't play his beloved violin.

I am brought out of my reverie by the sound of my son's voice calling up into the air. 'Justin, I hope you've finished your homework! You have an exam tomorrow!' Justin jumps with fright as he is brought crashing back down to reality.

'Yes Dad,' he grumbles. My grandson puts his violin down on the bed, a look of heaviness on his face. He scribbles something on the music score in pencil, moves his music stand to the side and heads toward his desk. The moment is broken. That wonderful veil between the worlds has been firmly closed, expectation taking its place.

My son is just like me. Always driven by what is 'right,' by the practical necessities of life. He supported Justin playing the violin when he was younger as he believed it would strengthen his mind, teach him discipline and lead him towards an under-standing of commitment to a solid future. It was meant to be a tool not a passion, but from the moment those ten-year-old hands picked up the instrument and scratched the bow across the strings something changed in Justin. The sound was atrocious! Like a cat being strangled. But slowly and surely the cat began to sing, and the nightingale escaped from its throat, a thing of true beauty emerging.

But beauty doesn't pay the bills, it doesn't pass maths exams, or English tests, and so it has been slowly pushed down, a tool no longer serving its purpose.

I don't blame my son. This is how I was raised, and how I raised him. But the sins of the father become the sins of the son. I want to speak to my son. To tell him what a mistake he is making! But I can't. I know this and yet for the first time since I left my body, I feel an urge to make a difference. Why didn't I see this before it was too late? I stand up and cross the room to look over my grandson's shoulder. Calculus is spread out before his eyes while his ears still hear musical notes. I kiss the top of his head, taking a moment to whisper in his ear. 'Never give up your dream. Find a way to be true to yourself. Do what you love. Be brave. The world needs you to be brave. Your soul is crying out for you to make a difference. I see that now. Hear it! Listen to it and do as it says! You, just as you are, with all your hopes and dreams and passions are what the world needs. Not another child seeing the world through his parent's eyes. See the world for what you believe it to be and it will become that. Never stop playing. Never stop feeling. Just be you.'

As I head towards his bedroom door, I take a last glance around his room. Posters of rock bands and pretty girls are placed next to famous classical musicians on his walls. I leave Justin encased by the light from his desk lamp, focusing on the books laid out before him. I hope he has heard me.

I walk out of the room and down the stairs. I see my son in

the kitchen preparing dinner. He will eat alone tonight. He will be sitting across the table from his child but neither will talk. I see such contrast between my son and my daughter. Such different personalities born out of the same place. How can two such different people be created from the same environment? I suppose it came from our placing different expectations on them during their childhood. He is a loving father and he wants the best for Justin. But we need to stop occasionally and connect and learn about the people we live with, the children we have created. We laugh when they are little as they recount their dreams of being princes or princesses, firefighters or police officers, dragon slayers or astronauts, and yet the imagination and passion we praise and encourage so much when they are little, we push away as they start to grow, not knowing how to develop dreams alongside growing bodies.

I put more pressure on my son than I did on my daughter. It was partly the era they were raised in, but it was partly the beliefs I picked up from my parents. A girl can grow into a mother, a wife, a homemaker, and yet a son needs to provide. How can he provide if he doesn't follow a traditional path? Is there a way to explore this, to encourage this branching out from expectation and towards something perhaps more rewarding? Certain cultures nowadays encourage the father to play a much more permanent role in the upbringing of their children. Paternity leave is taken with a sense of pride and worn as a badge of honour. Children grow up with an equal participation from both parents, learning so much more about the world through a double set of eyes than just one. Why can't the woman provide while the man stays at home and raises the children? Why can't they share these duties? I see society now as being slow to catch up. It's a shame really as so much could be gained from this new way of looking at things.

My son became a different person when I insisted he give up his sculpting. He seemed to lose a part of himself, but I was too busy, too 'right' to notice at the time. His behaviour changed, and I put it down to teenage angst but maybe he had needed that creative outlet, or perhaps it was a stronger part of his identity than I had realised. I ask myself now what I would have done with this realisation. Not much I suppose. Perhaps I didn't want to see, as I justified my decisions easily and effortlessly. But he lost touch with part of himself which I now see had a larger effect than I saw at the time. I don't want to over-think things, but I wonder if it affected his ability to be a father and a husband? He was not able to connect with his wife in the way she needed, in an emotional way. And I see that now with his son. He is out of touch. Disconnected. Wanting what's best for him but not knowing how to give it. Not knowing what it is that he needs to give.

I sit with my son and watch him cook. He never used to cook but the breakup of his marriage has led to new discoveries, some not so sought after. You never know what you've got till you lose it, or so they say. He had a good woman and he let her slip away. He was so focused on his career, and the visions of what lay ahead for his family, that he forgot to be with them in the very moment in which they needed him. He talked about building foundations for the future, making financial investments, working hard to get the promotions he needed in order to grow with the family's needs, to provide the right schooling for their son, the right house, the right environment, the right things. But what are things when there is no-one to share them with? Sure, my grandson could boast to his friends about the latest gadget that his father had brought back from one of his many business trips but it was a shallow joy, a put-on joy meant for other people.

My son never talked about it much, but I could see the strain his long hours in the office were putting on his marriage. He thought he was doing the right thing by his family, working for their security, but while my son's intentions kept him firmly in the future, his wife's needs were planted firmly in the present. What good is a future without the right present? The foundations need to be well built before you can progress.

My wife and I may not have always seen eye to eye, and not being the romantic type I wasn't always able to fulfil her emotional needs. But we shared a vision; a vision for our marriage, a vision for our family and a vision for our life, and this is what carried us through the hard times. We knew we were on the same page even if it didn't always feel like it. We could talk things through when need be, and we shared the same values.

I can't say that about my son and his ex-wife. I believe they probably started out that way, but life has a funny way of getting in the middle, and as careers and having a child and mismatching visions for the future took over, they weren't able to cope. Their marriage was not strong enough and they joined the ever-growing pool of statistics.

One thing I will give them credit for is that they never fought in front of Justin. They would wait until he was in bed or he was at school or at a friend's house before letting their emotions loose. But children aren't stupid. Justin could feel what was going on even if he couldn't see it.

He came to me one day and announced that he thought his parents were getting a divorce. Nothing had been said so it came as quite a shock to us. I immediately picked up the phone and asked my son to come over. I said it was urgent. When my son arrived we had a quiet talk in the kitchen, just the two of us, and there he confessed that yes indeed, he and his wife had agreed to separate. We then agreed that it was best to sit down and try to explain to Justin what was going on. We spoke to Justin like a man, forgetting he was only a child of nine years old.

He cried, my wife cried, but my son and I remained stoic. One staring at the floor, the other the wall. But there it was, unleashed, and it needed addressing. 'I want to go home,' my grandson said. So he was packed up in the car and off they drove. 'Home' would take on new meaning for my grandson over the next few months.

We can't blame ourselves when things go wrong. It is too easy to weigh ourselves down with guilt and pain and sorrow. Feelings need to be processed, time is needed to heal, and then the show must go on. Just like forgiveness, acceptance doesn't need to mean that you wanted something to happen or that you are OK with it. Acceptance is a crucial step in any difficult situation, because even if you want to change something, you need to first acknowledge that it exists. Acknowledgement and acceptance, I suppose I should say. The two seem to go together.

But my son and his then-wife handled things well and explained to Justin that the divorce was not his fault, that there was nothing he could have done to save the marriage and that sometimes these things just happen. I'm not sure if the last phrase gave him much comfort, but the first two certainly did. He saw a counselor and had time off school to process everything that was crumbling down around him. He learned strategies to help him pick the pieces up one by one and he realised, upon returning to school, that he was not the only one in this sinking boat. He realised that perhaps the boat wasn't sinking after all but was taking him towards the next stage of his life. A life split between two 'homes,' time split between two parents. Things started to look up for my grandson but then my son went back to his old ways and poor Justin was left behind.

We tend to return to habits and familiarity when uncertainty knocks on our door, and this is what my son chose to do. He too had felt adrift after the divorce, as if he lost a bit of himself with the sinking ship. He worked even harder, the long hours keeping him apart from Justin. Justin matured a lot shortly after the divorce, as he learned to look after himself emotionally as well as physically. He found solace in his music, he found escape, and he breathed it in like a fine perfume. But a child needs a childhood and too much pressure was placed on Justin's shoulders. I really hope they can work things out.

I stand up from the kitchen table feeling all of my seventy-eight years. I know there is nothing I can do here now, and that it is time to go, but I don't want to leave. I want to help my son somehow, I want to comfort him as I know he is hurting, as much, if not more than my grandson.

'I love you,' I tell my son, those words not often escaping from my mouth when I was alive. 'I see that you are doing your best, and I am proud of you, but you need to accept the situation now, and you need to see the damage that is being done to Justin. Find a way to re-connect with him, as you are both hurting and need to be there for each other. You have such an incredible son. Be proud of him! Show him that you are proud of him and of his passion and of his perseverance. See him for who he truly is. Accept him and love him as he is. Allow him to be. But don't forget to accept and love yourself. Be kind to yourself and be kind to Justin. Find a way to be there for him.'

I turn and head out of the kitchen feeling weighed down by sorrow, but I know things will work out. I have to believe it. They will both find their feet again and will find their rhythm. I just hope my son and my grandson felt my words.

I walk out of the house, on to the street and turn towards the main road. A cool breeze touches my face and helps to lift my spirits. A stroll in the fresh evening air will do me good I decide. With each step I take I breathe in deeply, feeling the sorrow slowly leave me with every bit of air that escapes my lungs. I see lights coming on in lounge room windows and cars wearily pulling into driveways after a long day. Birds are settling into their nests for the night, another long day of seeking, hunting and providing tucked neatly under their wings.

I turn the corner, passing a young woman walking an enormous dog, and the dog looks at me and sniffs the air. He pulls on the lead and plops his bottom down on the pavement, refusing to budge. He continues to look at me while his owner begs and pleads with him to get moving. 'Come on Axel!' she says. 'I want to go home! It's cold!' but Axel remains unmoved. I suppose he can sense me. Dogs do have a sixth sense, of that I'm certain. She pulls a dog biscuit out of her pocket and waves it in front of Axel's face. The distraction works and he chomps down the biscuit while happily trotting towards the next tree against which he will cock his leg. Dogs are such simple creatures and yet I think we could learn a lot from their happy abandon and relentless loyalty.

CHAPTER 10

The Dance Class

I AM NOW on the main street, heading towards the glowing warmth of the shop lights. It is dark and people are hurrying home from their busy days. I walk past the hairdressers and I notice music blaring out from the basement beneath. I head down the stairs, passing underneath a neon sign showing a pair of dancers moving back and forth. 'Hot Hips' is written on the sign and I decide to take a risk and go where I have never dared to go before.

As I enter the room I am overcome for a moment by the volume of the music. It is deafening! Couples sway back and forth, spinning away from each other to then swing quickly back. Hips swiveling, skirts swooshing and heels spinning. The teacher is leading the way at the front of the class but occasionally walks around the room, correcting posture or pushing hips closer together. He speaks with an accent I can't quite place and walks with a posture that can only mean years of dancing. He is a thing of beauty, a statue of David in a black shirt and tight trousers.

I watch as the couples stand next to each other, each taking a step forward and then immediately stepping back, as if they have changed their mind about the direction they want to go in. Feet then start stepping sideways and again stepping back, arms moving in strange circular motions. Bodies then come together in perfect unison, male hips moving just as freely as female ones. I think this is what they call Salsa.

I decide to join in. I figure I don't have much to lose, as no-one can see me and there is no physical body to injure. I listen to the beat of the music and try to take a step, but I miss the beat and have to stop and listen again. I try to let my non-physical body react to the music, to sway to the beat, but the last time I danced was at my wedding, and it was only in reaction to one-too-many drinks and a penny placed in the duke box. I listen again, this time deciding to let my nodding head find the beat. 'Right, off we go!' I say to myself as my feet start to move. But I'm completely out of rhythm.

I start to laugh as I imagine how foolish I must look right now. I imagine the faces of my family as they stare, eyes unbelieving, towards their tightly-stitched father, the accountant, the man who clearly wasn't hiding a talent for salsa dancing! I laugh and laugh. Oh it feels great! I feel so free and suddenly I don't care that I can't keep the beat, that my two left feet have met my two left hips! It just feels so liberating to be surrounded by people who are loving what they are doing, to let the music float over us and through us and to give our bodies over to magical notes.

I move my arms like a train with two wheels moving at opposite beats, the movement naturally making my shoulders move. I stay with this for a while as I feel my body being led by the music. Next, I start to sway my hips, my eyebrows knitted with concentration and intent. Then comes the tricky part. I start to move my feet, one behind the other and then back again, the return signaling to the other foot to move backwards. The couples in front of me start to bounce their hips up and down as their legs move out to the side and back again. It's all I can do not to fall over and I again find myself laughing out loud. I feel absolutely ridiculous and it feels wonderful! For the first time in my life I am laughing at myself, and it is so liberating! I decide to just go for it, turning circles on the spot and punching my arms in the air. I start spinning towards the wall, stop myself and decide to spin back to my starting point, like someone who has just miraculously regained the use of their legs. I bounce up and down on the spot, not caring if I am bouncing to the beat of the music or not, and I tip my head back and laugh out loud again.

I decide to spin around and through the couples, feeding off their energy and giving them mine. I see the connection that the dancing has brought each of them, and feel the music knitting their souls together. Dancing to music is such a wonderful thing. Children innately understand this, and don't let inhibitions stop them from throwing themselves into it whole heartedly, like a crystal clear swimming pool just begging them to dive in.

There comes an age of course where they suddenly become acutely aware of the adults watching and smiling at them, and so they get shy and stop, but until that moment they are lost in the most wonderful world of colourful music weaving itself around compliant limbs.

I feel just like a child as I float through the room, oblivious to anything but the music, the fast-moving couples and my own feelings of pure joy and weightlessness. It feels so good to let myself be free. To shed those years of inhibitions and embarrassment and just to give myself fully to the moment.

I decide to take a break and so I sit down on the floor with my back against the wall. As I look around the room I notice shiny new shoes and old worn-out ones. I notice designer handbags and plastic shopping bags. I see high-quality feather and down winter coats and cheaper synthetic ones. The room really is full of all walks of life weaving together in a solidarity and oneness that comes from a shared passion or belief.

I watch the couples, examining each of their faces and wondering who they are. One girl really stands out to me. It is not her bleach-blonde hair with the long dark roots, or the scruffy-toed dancing shoes she wears. Nor is it the hole in her tights nor the red and black check shirt vying for my attention. It is the intensity with which she dances, a look of total concentration and utter bliss on her face. She is completely lost in the moment, any thoughts of a bleak future or not enough money in the bank waiting in the cold outside where she left them.

There has been a lot of talk about meditations and mindfulness lately. I always thought that the term mindfulness was misleading as I thought the point was to empty the mind and not to keep it full? But the message itself is pretty clear; focus on the now, you only have the present. The past is gone and the future is yet to be written, no matter what our negative thoughts and possessing ego have to say about it. We can only do something now. Make the most of now. The present is a gift as they say, and the word play appeals to my sense of humour. I have a chuckle as it dawns on me that I am seeing this before me right now. I suppose salsa dancing could be a kind of meditation or mindfulness in its own right. Any hobby that brings you joy, takes your mind away from cares and allows you to focus on this very moment must be not only good for the soul but good for the emotional and physical well-being of the participant. I'm starting to sound like a pop-psychologist but this is something I see so clearly now.

I feel this is why mobile phones are causing so much concern. My wife and I didn't go out to restaurants often, but when we did it astounded me to see how many young people (and those not so young) would be sitting at the table, surrounded by good friends and loved ones and they would be on their phones. As if something on social media is more important than being in that moment with those they care about! I remember once walking into a restaurant with my wife for our wedding anniversary and feeling annoyed that we were seated next to a very large group of people. Birthday balloons were tied to the backs of the chairs and bottles of wine were placed along the large table. I was about to ask if we could move to a quieter setting when my wife said to me 'Darling, none of them are talking! They are all too absorbed with their phones. No-one has even noticed us sit down.' I was shocked.

The waiter brought out their meals and one by one a phone was held in front of the plate of food and a photo was taken. Conversation started up at this point as I suppose it was easier to talk than scroll while eating. But it left a heaviness in my heart to see such young people full of promise and life to not be living it. What message was it sending to themselves and their friends that no-one was important enough for them to put down their phones?

I remember the advent of smart phones when I was working at the firm, getting close to retirement. What had been a delight of technology soon became a nuisance as people would enter the meeting room, heads glued to their phones, grunting a quick hello and going back to whatever world they were currently living in. The meeting would start, and phones would be placed firmly on the table, as if a status of some symbol I could never quite figure out. Importance? Busyness? I'm not sure, but it sent a message to the room that 'I am here because you asked me to be, but I am not going to give you my full attention.' What was so important that a phone could not be packed away or turned off during a one-hour meeting? The world certainly wasn't going to end, and the unanswered emails certainly weren't going to go anywhere, and as the years went on and I noticed more and more stress around me, I couldn't help but wonder if this constant need to be switched on and connected wasn't the cause of it.

I look back at the room of dancers and feel a rising of hope. There are no mobile phones in sight here, no minds anywhere other than where they need to be right now. Perhaps the world isn't so doomed after all! Perhaps there is hope for the next generation, as a new way will be found to incorporate technology and connectedness into a healthier way of living. Connectedness has taken on new meaning with the invention of the smart phone, but at its roots is a very important lesson for us all. Human beings are supposed to be connected, but be connected in the moment, together, sharing energy and a smile and face-to-face conversation with each other. People may feel they are connected when they share a 'like' on their social media account, and yet we are lonelier than ever. It's the art of small talk that is disappearing.

I remember sitting on the bus next to a colleague I didn't know very well. Everyone around us had their heads down, faces engaged with their phones, but for some reason she didn't. She opened up to me that day about how her father was sick and how she was worried about asking for time off work. We connected that day, as trite as that sounds, and while I walked home with a slight spring in my step as I felt I had helped her, it wasn't until we found ourselves at a company-wide presentation a few weeks later that the effect became apparent. It was such a simple thing but again as people were lost to their mechanical worlds waiting for the presentation to start, I caught her eye, walked up to her and asked how her father was doing. A tear came to her eye as she placed her hand on my arm and thanked me for asking and said he was doing much better. 'What's happened to your father?' someone next to her asked, and as I walked off I heard her tell the story she had needed to tell, and another small but significant connection was made.

It feels like years since that happened, and I haven't seen her since, but something I dismissed and soon forgot about has resurfaced for me now and I can see its true significance.

I look back around the room and I notice a rather shy-looking, elegantly-dressed woman in her thirties. She is immaculately turned out, dressed all in black and with a red and black tasseled shawl tied around her waist. Her low-heeled shoes look professional, but her body movements give her away. She does not remove her eyes from the floor very often, and her movements are tight as if her confidence hasn't found her yet. I look over to where I saw her place her bag earlier and conclude that she is most likely to be wealthy. She is very attractive, is slim and her makeup has been applied with care. She should be brimming with confidence and yet, here she is, slightly uptight and certainly uncomfortable, and I think that one can never know what is truly going on inside another. We make assumptions about ourselves and others, and with repetition these become our beliefs, but these beliefs are false! Why do we do ourselves such a disservice?

A light in the corner of the room is flickering and as it draws my attention away from the dancers, I notice the paint peeling off the ceiling. The once-white walls are marked, and the chairs scattered around the room have certainly seen better days. But it doesn't matter. No-one notices as they throw themselves head-first into their passion with true abandon.

I decide to get up and join them again and twirl in between an older couple. 'You look beautiful,' the man whispers to his partner, and she truly does. Her face is relaxed, her body is flowing and she doesn't have a care in the world. I hope she can carry this feeling with her as it really is infectious!

The music stops and the class comes to an end. Sweaty foreheads are wiped by tired arms, and cold water is poured down thirsty throats. There is an energy in the room that I can't quite describe but it is captivating and uplifting and needs to be shared with the world! I feel drunk on happiness and exhilaration, and smile at each couple as they say their goodbyes and their 'See you next week's and leave the room. What a gift to give oneself! The gift of movement and dance and pure in-the-moment happiness that will create feelings of lightness that will carry them through until the next day, if not until their next lesson. Who cares what one looks like? Who cares if you can't keep the beat! I realise now that no-one would have judged me for letting loose from time to time, so long as I did it with a full smile and a willing heart. That's why we smile at children, as we watch them totally absorbed in the moment, in whatever it is they are doing, living that moment with the concentration and whole-heartedness it deserves. Living today like it is their last, but never realising it. Adults have so much to learn from children, and so much to give each other. The gift of freedom to be who you want and need to be is invaluable but completely undervalued in today's world.

I watch as the teacher wipes down his face with a towel, takes the CD out of the player and puts it away in its case. He takes a long, well-earned drink from his water bottle, takes his dance shoes off and puts on boots. A warm coat is added to the ensemble and he walks towards the lights. As he turns them off and heads out the door and up the stairs back into reality, I wonder what his parents think of his choice of profession. Is he living their dream or is he one of those lucky people whose dreams are being lived without being tied down by parental obligation?

I walk back up the stairs and to the street, where I float off down the road, bouncing and twirling and singing to myself, having the time of my life.

After a few more minutes I find myself twirling to a stop outside a large supermarket. It stands exactly where my wife's family's grocery shop used to sit. I remember the day that her parents announced to us that a large supermarket chain had offered them a much-needed chunk of money to buy them out and they had accepted. My wife was devastated as she saw all her parents' hard work and dreams being flushed away. But who are we to stand in the way of progress? Certainly not my wife's family, nor the butcher's shop next door to them, nor the fish monger next to him. They all sold up and quickly got out of the way of the bulldozers as their lives were razed to the ground to soon be replaced with a different future.

So much has changed in my lifetime. So much progress has been made. I remember sitting down in my neighbour's house to watch the moon-landing. It may have been many decades ago but I remember it like it was yesterday. Five families crowded into the tiny living room all vying for the best spot in front of the black and white TV. The excitement was palpable as we watched something that had been completely inconceivable up until then actually unfold before our eyes. The world took on a different meaning for me in that moment with the realisation that perhaps anything really can happen. Perhaps I could even travel in space!

I kept newspaper cutouts of the moon landing and associated stories about Neil Armstrong and Buzz Aldrin as a way of reminding myself that anything is possible. I heard that Buzz Aldrin struggled to adjust to life back on earth after that incredible experience. He didn't like the limelight he was thrust into nor the position he was given in the airforce upon his return. No-one really knew what to do with him, and he didn't know what to do with himself and he felt completely lost and hopeless. Depression and the bottle were his only comforts for a long time after that world-changing moment, which leads me to think about how we tend to abandon our heros once we have taken what we need from them.

For me it was a dream that I eventually started to move away from, hopes for an exciting future starting to meld with the realities of an average one. I am OK with that, and I don't think I was ever cut out to be an astronaut, but I realise now that magic can sit next to reality and incredible things can be born when the two are allowed to merge.

A car horn startles me back to the supermarket and I move off down the street mumbling to myself about manners and people-these-days.

I let my mind wander as I feel the lingering after-effects of the salsa class carry me down the road. Most of my life I have missed the beauty in the small things, missed the opportunity to experience life at a deeper level. Why didn't I take a salsa class with my wife or let my astronautical dream last a little longer? I know I looked after my family to the best of my abilities and I really shouldn't regret anything, but I can't help but feel that I missed out on things.

CHAPTER 11

The Boss

WE ALL HAVE dreams and aspirations and some of us are better at going after them than others. We live in fear of scarcity, fear of never having enough, but few of us are brave enough to try to change that. We work in jobs that don't satisfy us because at least we get a steady pay cheque. We don't believe ourselves to be better than our current situation, and we don't strive to go after the sparks of inspiration that occasionally come our way. Inspiration eventually stops coming as we are too afraid to bring into creation the ideas it brings to us.

I was like that in life. I had a good job, a very good job, that covered our daily needs with a little bit left over every month. It was the perfect middle-class lifestyle and while we didn't have a lot of luxuries, we were able to provide the children with what they needed and then a little more. Was I happy in my job? At times, yes. I was with the company my whole working life and saw many changes, some good, others not so good, but I came to accept that things change and life moves on, and one must accept the good with the bad. Looking back on that view now, I realise how restrictive it was, how it can stop one from living one's life in accordance with their true purpose. I feel I was able to contribute to society through the job I performed every day but did I make a major difference to people's lives? Probably not. I know I certainly didn't make a major difference to my own life, but it was a good solid job and I earned an honest living and what more can one really want, I used to think.

But certainty can be shaken up at any moment, and that's what happened the day my new boss started. We were told we were to receive a new team member from the City, who had had a short but successful career as a trader and had now moved out our way with his young family in search of a change of pace. I liked the openness of this confession, as it made the man seem human.

The first day went very well. I was part of a team of eleven people and Peter was to head up our division. He was younger than I was, by a good ten years I would have guessed, but that didn't bother me. So long as he had the experience and the competence to lead our team, then age did not matter. We had our first team meeting mid-morning, after he had had his introductions with the CEO and the Board of Directors. He seemed slightly stressed but I suppose that's how one feels after a two-hour introduction meeting to the head team of the company.

Peter told us about himself and said he wanted to spend time with each of us over the next week getting to know us, our history with the company, and our aspirations. When it was my turn to meet with him, I ensured I went along prepared with notes about previous projects he needed to get up to speed on, as well as previous company presentations that I thought would help him understand how our team fitted into the wider company. I was, after all, the most senior member of the team in terms of experience, seniority and years with the company and I thought I would be able to help him settle in and get up to date as quickly as possible.

I sat down opposite Peter in his office. He had chosen to remain behind his desk rather than move us to the couch and the armchair that occupied the corner. I found that odd but I soon shrugged it off. He then started to ask me all sorts of questions about my life, my goals and what my five- and ten-year vision was for my career. I hesitated while I thought how best to answer this line of questioning. I was a bit taken aback as I didn't have the kind of vision he was asking about. I took a deep breath and lent back in my chair to think.

'Come on, I don't have all day,' he said. 'You either have goals or you don't.' He looked at me with chin slightly down towards his chest as if looking over the top of imaginary glasses. He was a big man, an ex-rugby player I had heard, and I must admit his size was slightly intimidating. His hands were placed on the desk in front of him, crossed in front of his enormous chest. I continued to stare at his hands while I tried to get my brain to work. How was he getting to me like this? Why was I now feeling so nervous?

He spread his hands suddenly, in an exasperated gesture, and then slapped them down on the desk. I jumped.

'At the age of sixteen,' he continued 'I had already decided which university I would attend, what age I would finish my degree, where I would work in my first professional job, at what age I would get married and at what age I would have both of the two children I had already planned to have. I met my now-wife during the year I said I would, and we had our first child at twenty-seven and our second child at twenty-nine, at... guess what... the exact ages I had already decided upon. If you don't grab life and tell it what you want, you will end up with nothing, a nobody, and that is a waste of everybody's time.' He sat back in his chair continuing to challenge me with his eyes.

I nervously opened my mouth to speak. 'I... I suppose I have always believed in working hard and then rewards would come when they were due. Promotions would arrive when I had proved myself beyond doubt of being capable, which is what I have achieved several times since being with the company.' My response came out stammered and I could feel the heat rising in my face.

He looked like a giant father looking down on his very disappointing son, a look of 'Why do I bother with you?' written all over his face. The man didn't even know me! Needing to turn the situation around quickly, with shaking hands I pulled out the presentations I had brought for him, and handed them over, briefly explaining what they were. He took them and immediately cast them aside, saying he would look if he had time later. He laid out very clearly what his expectations were for the team and for me and said he didn't suffer fools gladly. Was he calling me a fool, I asked myself? What had I done to deserve such wrath when we had only just met?

When I was dismissed, I stood up slowly, pushing back my chair in a stupor. As I left his office I turned around and asked if he wanted me to leave his door open.

'Close it!' he barked at me, never lifting his eyes from his computer screen. I went back to my desk, and heavily sat down in my chair. I was in shock and feeling slightly nauseous, as if I had just witnessed a terrible accident.

'How did it go?' whispered my colleague Amanda. She was holding her breath, eyes big and full of expectation. Her meeting with the new boss was coming up next.

'Um, I don't really know,' I answered honestly. 'He was a bit abrupt and direct I suppose and wanted to know what I had planned for my life and what my goals were. I would recommend you use the time now to prepare some.' I told her, leaving her to sit back at her desk to create a life plan in less than three minutes.

When Amanda came back out of her meeting she looked pale and shaken. I asked if she wanted to get a cup of tea and she gratefully said yes, so we headed to the kitchenette to put the kettle on.

'What a horrible man!' she exclaimed, a little too loudly.

'Sshh,' I said. 'You don't want him to hear you!'

'But how can he speak to people like that?' she asked, eyes moist with tears threatening to fall. 'He told me that he didn't have time for unmotivated people and that he would be watching us over the next few weeks to see who needs a shakeup. I feel like he was threatening me. It was most unpleasant!' Amanda fell silent, holding her mug close to her chest in her two hands, the warmth seeping through the ceramic providing her with a small comfort.

The next few weeks proved fairly uneventful as Peter was preoccupied with learning the ropes and meeting with the other divisions. He had a few work trips to do and so was away from the office a large part of the time. But one day he called a team meeting and told us to bring a project update to share with the team.

We all sat down quietly but nervously in the meeting room waiting for Peter to make his entrance. He walked to the front of the room, placed his two large hands down on the table in front of him and leant on them. He looked slowly around the room to see if he had everyone's attention. Suddenly the door opened and in walked Gemma, one of our junior accountants, a look of quiet terror on her face. Unfortunately, the only spare chair was at the front of the room and as she walked past the staring faces of her equally terrified teammates and took her seat at the front of the room, she mumbled an apology for being late.

'I DO NOT TOLERATE LATENESS!' Peter's deep voice boomed, eyes glaring at poor Gemma. He left his piercing eyes resting on her reddened face for a few seconds longer, letting his point sink in, and then turned to the rest of us and started the meeting.

Once Peter had taken us through his team rules that he expected all of us to follow, it was then our turn to go around the room with an update for the team on what we were working on and any obstacles we believed were standing in the way of achieving our goals.

When it came to my turn, I cleared my throat nervously, feeling tension rising up my back like cold fingers, that then settled into the base of my neck and dug into my spine. Why was I so tense around this man? Why did he terrify me so? Here I was, a grown man, older than Peter and with certainly much more life experience, and yet he had reduced me to a blubbering child!

Then came poor Gemma's turn. Having already been scolded once in the meeting, she had started off on shaky ground and I could see that her confidence was waning. As she started to talk through her topics for the meeting, Peter interrupted her and started challenging her on some of her numbers. It really put poor Gemma on the spot and I felt terribly sorry for her. She mumbled a few answers but was shot down each time.

'Enough! Stop! I've heard enough.' Peter spat. 'To be late to the meeting is one thing, but to come unprepared is another!'

'I'm s-s-sorry,' she said. 'I didn't bring the printout with me as I didn't think I would need it.' She looked down and I could see her wringing her hands under the table.

'Let's just move on,' Peter said, disappointment and what felt like loathing in his voice. What had we done to deserve this? We were what I would consider a high-performing team but ever since Peter had come on board I could see that team performance dipping and the morale that had once been fantastic, had seeped out of every one of us and evaporated into thin air. The meeting drew to an end and everyone left quietly, the silence speaking volumes.

Not everyone in the team was affected as badly as others, but no-one enjoyed having Peter as a boss. A few of the team members seemed to perform better with each meeting, as they knew what was expected of them and they made sure they prepared exactly what Peter wanted to hear. They knew their numbers as they memorised them before each meeting, wasting precious time on trying to please a very displeased god, afraid of the lightning bolts he could throw down at them from the sky.

Peter took great pleasure out of arriving unannounced at someone's desk and demanding the latest share price of a particular product our company sold or what position our company held on the ever-changing stock market. Numbers that did not need to be memorised but which he used as a way of keeping us small and terrified and firmly in our places. We weren't allowed to look the number up, even if we had them printed out in front of us. We had to memorise them every morning and hope and pray that we still remembered them by lunchtime. If you didn't know all your latest numbers, he would bark 'Not good enough!' and walk away shaking his over-sized head. In my opinion it took our focus off what we should have been doing and kept us tied to our desks out of fear. Fear does not sustain us, it wears us down and takes away our precious energy and our hope for the future.

As time went on I realised that Peter was clearly in over his head. He had been given a lot of responsibility, with a large team working in an area he was not completely familiar with. He had a lot to learn, but rather than rely on the team and help them in order to help himself, he chose to project his fear on to us and build himself up by bringing us down. Why couldn't he see that he is only as good as his team? If the team shone, he shone, and yet he seemed to believe that if he made out that we were all a bunch of imbeciles any failed results could be shifted on to us, and he could simply shrug his shoulders as if to say 'Look what I have to work with.'

He used to steal our work. It started off innocently enough; he would ask us to prepare a presentation for him, usually for the following day without much warning. We were never present at these meetings, so we assumed that we would at least get some of the credit. But one day Peter was asked to present at a company-wide meeting, and this was the first time that we saw him in such a situation. He walked up to the stage, and his face cracked into a very unfamiliar and unbecoming smile, as if the muscles had to remember which position they were supposed to go into. He looked more like an ogre than a man, but I suppose that is rather unkind of me. Still, that is how I remember him. On went the screen and up went his slides, and to the team's horror, he assumed full responsibility for all the work and successful quarterly results he presented that afternoon, giving absolutely no credit to his hard-working team who had made it happen. We all sat there in seething silence as the audience clapped their thanks and he went and sat back down in the front row, a job well done.

We used to have mixed feelings towards any meetings where Peter's boss would be present, as the lead up to those meetings was always dreadful, but the meetings themselves were very relaxed as he was always so charming to us in front of the Vice President. She never saw the truth, only the façade of a wonderfully well-coordinated team who were incredibly lucky to have such a caring boss.

One day, Gemma came to see me. She asked if we could slip into one of the meeting rooms and have a quick chat about something. When I sat down she asked me directly and bluntly what I thought of Peter. I was guarded in my response as, even though I knew Gemma had been having a hard time with him, I didn't trust the man and didn't know who to trust in the team anymore. I wanted to protect my own back.

'He is a tough boss but I suppose that is what we need,' is how I answered the question. Gemma sat back looking defeated.

'But you see how he treats us? We are treated worse than a piece of chewing gum stuck on the bottom of his shoe! I have had enough and I want to go and see his boss and tell her the truth of what is going on. I am talking to the team on a one-to-one basis and I want to see who will join me. Are you in?' Gemma asked.

I thought for a moment, wondering what I should do. On the one hand I could join Gemma and support her in trying to get rid of this vile creature who had taken over our team, but on the other hand, I could lose my job in the process. I had a family to feed and a mortgage to pay and so I made my decision.

'I'm sorry Gemma. I salute your bravery and think you are making the right decision to go to the top, but I have too much at stake and need this job. You are young and can find another job if things don't work out, but I am not as flexible as you.' I sighed and then fell silent. I felt enormous guilt welling up inside me but I had my family to think of.

Gemma opened an angry mouth and spoke again. 'Fine, you are just like the rest of them. I thought that out of the whole team, you are the one I could rely on but I suppose I will just have to do this on my own.' She stormed out of the room and disappeared in the direction of the Vice President's office.

An hour later, Gemma reappeared, face ashen and mascara streaked down her cheeks.

'What happened?' I stammered. 'What's wrong?!'

'I've lost my job that's what!' she snapped and with that Gemma started to cry. She went on to explain that the meeting had seemed to start off well. She was careful to not get too emotional when describing the situation with Peter and to remain as factual as possible. She said the Vice President listened intently, occasionally asking a question or for a point to be clarified. Then as the meeting felt like it was coming to a close, she received a reply that she had not been expecting. She was told that Peter was a star performer and that big things had been achieved since he had joined the company. Gemma was told in no uncertain terms that if there was a problem it lay with her, and that according to Peter, Gemma's performance had been below par lately. She was told that clearly she was not suited to the culture of the company and that due to that fact they would not be able to continue her contract. She should therefore go and say her goodbyes to the team, pack up her things and leave. She would be paid any outstanding holiday or overtime pay in her next and final pay cheque.

I was stunned. As I watched Gemma placing her belongings into a cardboard box, tears streaming down her face, I thought about how unfair the world can be. How can someone clearly not qualified to be a leader end up in such a position, and how had he managed to pull the wool over the management team's eyes? I decided then and there that something had to be done.

'I'm really sorry this happened to you Gemma. I will pick up the fight.' I said. I truly meant it. She nodded as she kept packing her things.

'Well, that's it,' she said a few minutes later. 'I have everything so I suppose I will go now. It's been nice working together. Please keep in touch,' she said quickly. With a sob, she turned and walked away, clutching the cardboard box to her chest as tightly as she could. She had to go and see HR and then would leave the office, never to return.

I sat there for a while in stunned silence. I felt a mix of emotions, each vying for the dominant position. Shame won in the end. How could I not have stood up beside her against our boss? But I felt shame at the relief I felt because I had not been the one to lose my job. Shame that again another person good at politics but not their job was able to win. Shame to work for a company that allowed their employees to be treated so badly. It was at this unfortunate moment that Peter decided to come over and talk to the team.

'Right, so you know what's happened. Gemma wasn't the best fit for us and so she has had to leave. It's a shame but we need to have a strong team and Gemma simply didn't fit the mould. Let's get back to work shall we?' and with that Peter walked off, completely unaffected by the life he had temporarily ruined. It was this callousness that sealed his fate. I stood up, grabbed a notepad and pen and went to a meeting room. I closed the door and spent the next two hours jotting down everything I could remember; all the atrocities Peter had produced, and the effect he was having on team morale. Sure, productivity may have been temporarily high, but it certainly wasn't sustainable, and we had already suffered the loss of another team member, in addition to Gemma, who had left simply because the strain was too much.

When my notes were finished, I took a deep slow breath, put my pen down, sat back in the chair and rubbed my eyes and then my face. What a complete and utter waste of energy, but I was no longer going to put up with this situation, even if it meant risking my financial security and that of my family. Leaving my notes on the table I stood up and headed towards Peter's office. I didn't knock but walked straight in and said I needed to talk to him. I wanted to speak in neutral territory so I took him back into the meeting room where my notes were waiting and shut the door. I told him to sit down as I wanted to talk to him about something. There must have been a strength to my voice that he hadn't heard before as he sat down with a puzzled look on his face.

My arms betrayed me as I sat down opposite him. They started to shake which then started a series of tremors all down my body. The stress of these recent times was too much and it was trying to break me. As I sat across the table from the man who had been bullying me and my team, it took all my strength not to reach across and punch him. I felt so angry for everything he had put us through, and even angrier that he didn't seem to care.

As I took him through my notes, and the accusations I held against him, I tried to keep my voice as calm as possible. It was even harder than I thought it would be to stand up to a bully, but as I had decided to throw everything on the line in the name of justice, I felt I had nothing left to lose.

When I finished going through my notes, I looked him in the eyes for the first time since we first sat down, a nauseous feeling settling hard in my stomach. He didn't say anything for a few minutes, but never took his eyes from my face, as if trying to read me and see how far I would really go. After what felt like forever, he broke the silence with two short sentences: 'I'm sorry that is how you feel. I will take your comments on board.'

What was I supposed to do with that?! I had no idea how he felt as he kept a poker face, and I couldn't read his body language. He calmly pushed his chair back, stood up and walked out of the room, leaving me alone. I started to panic as I didn't know what would happen next. I decided that I had to stay in control of this situation and so I went straight to HR.

After explaining the situation and the meeting I had just had with Peter, the HR Manager looked at me with great concern in her eyes. She explained the procedure to me, which included a face-to-face meeting with Peter, Peter's manager and myself. I was asked if I had any other witnesses who would join me in the meeting, and I shook my head, certain that people would be even more afraid to stand up to Peter now that Gemma had lost her job.

As I sat there listening to how sorry she was to hear about the situation and how it was up to me to do something about it, but that she would support me, I looked out the window at a flock of birds flying overhead. As they landed in a nearby tree, I started to wonder what it would be like to feel like them. To not have to face issues like this, and to just go about one's life doing what was necessary to survive and nothing else. Then the irony of that statement dawned on me. Surviving was what I was doing right now.

'I can only help you if you denounce him during a face to face meeting.' She continued, 'You must bring proof and lots of it. Better yet, if you can get some of your teammates to join you it would help your case tremendously.' She saw the look of hesitation on my face. 'I am trying to help you,' she said. 'I have seen this kind of behaviour in the past and I do not tolerate it, but protocol is protocol and everyone deserves a fair chance. While I believe you, I only have your side of the story and Peter's side needs to be heard too.'

I said I would think about it and told her I would come back to her the next day with my decision. I decided to first call the colleague who had left recently after the pressure got too much for him, and then I would gather the team for one more conversation about the matter and see if I could drum up some support.

The phone call proved to be very interesting and gave me the boost I needed. My ex-colleague had been very open in his exit interview about how badly Peter treated the team, including his plagiarism of other people's work. I wondered why nothing had been done and thought what a shame it was that this had had no positive effect on the situation with Gemma. Perhaps she would have been able to keep her job if the exit interview had been referenced?

Having already taken more steps than I thought I was brave enough to take, for the first time in a long time I felt truly proud of myself. I hoped that confronting Peter would mean that he would leave us alone now. All we wanted to do was get on with our jobs and not feel him breathing down our necks.

When Peter was out of the office the next morning, I took the opportunity to hold a meeting with the team. I brought them up to speed with everything that had happened since Gemma had left and the conversations I had recently had. I asked if there was anyone willing to sit with me during the meeting with HR. No-one said anything. I tried again, this time taking a different approach and offering to be the spokesperson, and to lead the meeting. Still, there were no offers of support. I could understand. I had done the same to Gemma. So I took it upon myself to stand up to the bully like I had never managed to do in my school days, and blast the consequences. Bullies lose their power when their victims get up and fight and that was exactly what I intended to do.

I went home and spoke again to my wife, to ensure I still had her full support. The end result could be bad for our family situation and it was only fair that she got a say in the matter. She told me to go 'rip him to shreds', to use her exact words and that is exactly what I set out to do as I headed into work the next day.

However, as I got closer to the office, my stomach started to do somersaults and my confidence started to drain. I tried to picture what would happen in my mind, and each time all I could see was a negative result. I like to think of myself as a rather cool, calm and collected sort of chap, but that morning I was not even close. I felt like a nervous wreck by the time I got to my desk, not knowing whether I had the strength to go through with it.

I went to the kitchenette to make myself a calming cup of tea and I noticed two of my teammates standing nervously just behind me. As I turned to look at them, Greg opened his mouth and in a quiet voice said 'We have been talking, Emma and I, and we have decided to join you in the meeting today.'

My heart could have burst for joy! My body jumped with the news, hot tea spilling over the side of my mug. I didn't care. I couldn't feel it as I was so happy to have the support of some of my teammates. They both smiled at me nervously, clearly just as terrified as I was. But now I had others to be strong for and it boosted my confidence to no end.

When the meeting time came, I nodded to Emma and Greg and the three of us stood up from our desks and headed towards the lift to go up to the boardroom where the meeting was to take place. The rest of the team lifted their heads and as I made eye contact with a few of them they smiled their support, and I knew I couldn't blame them for not joining us. Their sense of survival had kicked in and their fear was leading the way.

We walked into the room, Emma and Greg walking a few paces behind me. 'You can do this, you can do this' I kept saying in my mind over and over. My knees felt weak, my stomach contained a whole kaleidoscope of butterflies and my mouth was as dry as a desert. But I knew I was doing the right thing, no matter what the result ended up being.

The head of HR started the meeting by thanking everyone for taking the time to discuss such an important matter. She noted for the minutes all who were present, with a slight surprise in her voice when she noted Emma and Greg. I thought I saw a tiny smile on her face when she said their names, but I could have imagined it.

The meeting lasted exactly ninety minutes, with quite a few heated moments and fierce rebuttals. But when I had said all I had come to say, and my teammates had been asked to comment as well, I finally found the courage to look Peter directly in the eye. His face was red, his shoulders were slumped and for the first time since he started with the company he looked utterly defeated. His gaze was downcast and his hands were in his lap. A tiny part of me felt sorry for him, never truly knowing why he had taken the path of the bully rather than the role of supportive manager he could have easily chosen.

Peter, Greg, Emma and I were asked to leave the room and we left the Head of HR and the Vice President of Finance and Sales to discuss our fate.

'Thanks for nothing,' was all Peter could mumble when we left the room. I slowed my pace and let him get ahead of me, not knowing what to say, nor wanting to speak. I felt exhausted, anxious, but somehow also at peace as I knew I had been brave, had stood up for justice and had done my absolute best.

We went back to work and tried to focus as best we could for the next couple of days while we waited to hear what the fallout would be. At the end of that week I came into work and my team members who were already in the office were standing around talking and laughing and looking like they could walk on air.

'What are you all grinning about?' I asked, smiling myself as I picked up on their happiness.

'He's gone. You did it. YOU DID IT! You got rid of the bastard and now we can get on with our lives and not live in fear anymore!' one of my teammates said, grinning from ear to ear. 'He's moved out of his office. We don't know what's happened but there is a meeting this morning with HR and the VP. We will find out then. But we are all still here and you did it!' He pulled me into a fierce hug of brown bear proportions, nearly crushing my slight frame in the process and bumping my glasses askew.

At ten o'clock, we all gathered again in the boardroom, a strange feeling settling in my stomach as I walked back on to the battleground. We all sat around the table and waited for the meeting to start. Peter's boss stood up and thanked us all for coming. She told us that Peter had decided to take up another opportunity within the company in a different department. We would not be seeing him at this office anymore but could still reach him on email if we were interested in contacting him.

We were told that recruitment for a new department head would take place in due course and in the meantime, we were to report into her.

We all tried to contain our excitement, but when we left the room, and were out of earshot a few fists happily punched the air and a few whoops of delight escaped smiling mouths. We agreed that we would go and have a celebratory drink together that night after work. Now I am not normally one to drink on a school night, so-to-speak, but this occasion was a true cause for celebration!

When I got back to my desk after the meeting, I picked up the phone and called Gemma to tell her the news. She was very happy to hear what had happened and relieved that justice had been served. While we didn't know what role he had been moved into, we had been told that he would be managing a much smaller team and would be sent on a course to learn effective team management skills. I invited Gemma to join us for drinks but she gracefully declined. I could understand that, and it was simply good to hear that she had moved into a fantastic role after she left our company, one that really suited her and made her very happy.

I do not hold a grudge against Peter and I certainly don't wish him ill will. I just hope that he learned a valuable lesson about team management; we are all human after all. As for me, I learned a lot about myself during that very stressful time. I learned that I really could stand up for myself, that I had courage and that I was able to fight for justice no matter the consequences or the fear that was trying to hold me back. While I haven't found Peter to say goodbye, I don't feel I need to. I do wish him well, however, and hope that he found his feet as well as the peace that must have been missing from his life.

CHAPTER 12

The Wife

I HAVE NOW come to the final person that I want to say goodbye to. I have saved the best until last as they say. I want to savour this last goodbye to the only person who truly understood me and who devoted her life to supporting mine. What were her dreams as she wiped yet another snotty nose and kissed yet another grazed knee? As she provided yet another meal and collapsed on the sofa each evening after the kids had gone to bed. She never really said much but I could see the tiredness on her face at night as she crawled into bed exhausted from yet another day managing our family. I never really understood the true significance of this. I had had a long day in the office and I felt tired. When I clocked out each day at 5 o'clock and walked to the bus stop I thought about how nice it will be to get home and put my feet up and relax. I had spent the day providing for the family and now I deserved to come home and relax and recharge for the next day ahead.

I suppose I took for granted the way her body moved slower in the evenings than it did in the mornings. How her posture had changed over the years and what carrying a toddler on one hip while attending to a crying baby on the other day-in-day-out could do to a person. She adored her children and adored us, I knew that, but I never stopped to wonder how tiring her day had been, how much sacrifice she had made in order to make other people happy.

I am back in our street now and stand gazing at the house in which we raised our children and shared our lives together. To where we lived through challenges that life threw at us from time to time and to where we celebrated moments in life that we shared. I walk up the path towards the front door for the last time, and I linger outside a moment longer, taking one final look around. The moon is shining on the newly-wet grass and is casting an eerie glow across the street.

I walk through the front door and take a final look around the lower floor of the house. Photos of four generations line the hallway walls and I follow these down towards the kitchen. The lights are off as it is time for my wife to go to bed, but I see paintings and tiny handprints on paper attached to the fridge and tomorrow's to-do list written on the white board stuck to the kitchen wall. I glance one more time at the oven that has cooked our family meals for the last thirty years and the washing machine, a more recent addition, that has washed all our clothes. I turn and head back up the hallway, keen to be next to my wife one last time.

As I enter our bedroom, I look at the photo on our wall that was taken the day our son started kindergarten. We all look at the camera smiling, painting the perfect picture of a happy and relaxed family, but I remember the stress behind that photo, how nervous we had been as our son approached his first day of school. He was always a sensitive boy, always one to get upset if another child bumped him accidently and didn't say sorry, just like our granddaughter. He took everything personally and I suppose that rubbed my wife and me up the wrong way and made us worry about how he would get through life. We took quite a tough stance with him, perhaps not allowing his true emotions to shine through enough. We would brush aside his tears as if crumbs from the breakfast table, believing that we needed to toughen him up to face the cruel harsh world.

My wife would lie awake at night often wondering if we were doing the right thing. 'What if we just let him be?' she would ask. 'What if we trust in our abilities as parents to bring our children up in the best way possible, while allowing them to be who they need to be. Why do we have to make them fit the mould?' I would wonder that too as I reflected on yet another tense moment with my son as I reacted negatively to his tears.

He came home one day from playing at the neighbour's and he was very upset. I could see he was frustrated and angry and hurt but he refused to talk about it. He was only six at the time but I expected him to think and act like an adult. I asked him what was wrong and he mumbled something under his breath and went and slumped down on the couch. I told him that if he was going to be moody then he could take his mood to his bedroom and not come out until he could find a better one. He stomped up the stairs and slammed his bedroom door. I chased after him, opened his door and said that he could stay in there for even longer for having a bad attitude. I went back downstairs, made myself a cup of tea and sat down to read the paper. My wife had taken our daughter to ballet class and I sat in the kitchen and waited for them to come home before I told my son he could come out of his bedroom.

His face was pale from crying and his head was held low. My wife asked what had happened and he silently started to cry again. 'Oh great,' I said. 'Here we go again.' But my wife lent down, put her hands on his shoulders and asked him what was wrong.

'It's just that Andrew wouldn't let me have a turn of his Pacman game and would only let me watch. I got upset and so he said I could finally have a go but he kept telling me I was doing the wrong thing and so I got up and left. He was not nice to me and it made me feel bad!' He burst into tears again and my wife put her arms lovingly around him and let him have his moment. When his tears subsided, she asked if he wanted to help her prepare dinner and he nodded, and I saw his shoulders relax as they went off together to prepare the evening meal.

Perhaps I should have been kinder to him. Perhaps I should have allowed him to express his feelings a bit more and not worry so much about the future I was preparing him for but instead focus on the very moment when he needed me. I thought I was doing the right thing by toughening him up and thinking about his future and what I thought he needed, and while I think he turned out pretty well, I see now that a loving hand, or a kind word can make much more of a long-term difference to a child than a tough reaction and a stiff upper lip.

My wife had so much more patience than me. She was, and still is, a very loving mother. But she judged herself all the time. She constantly pitched herself against the ideal of the perfect parent. Her aim was to never lose her temper, to always be available for the children and to always treat them with the utmost patience and respect. She naturally failed at this and would berate herself nearly every night as she held up visions of her perfect ideal and saw how short she came. She constantly told herself she could do better, that tomorrow she would be better, more patient, more kind, less in a hurry and less demanding. Tomorrow she would not raise her voice or lose her patience or speak to the children crossly. She would lovingly coax the toddler into her coat rather than shoving it on her with brute force as they rushed out the door. She would sit on the floor and play cars and trucks for hours with her son, leaving aside the washing and the millions of chores she really needed to get on with.

And yet tomorrow would come and she would fall back into what she viewed as bad habits. The toddler would scream and kick as she tried to put winter boots on her tiny feet when all she wanted to wear was summer sandals. Our son would spill his milk down his freshly washed T-shirt as he again slurped milk from his cereal bowl (where he picked up this habit I shall never know). She knew that if she didn't get out the door by 8.15 they would be late to school, and that would not fit with her perfect mother image. She would feel the heat rising in her body and manifesting in her face as she rushed around trying to find the missing school shoe or as she pulled the half-eaten and very squashed banana out of our son's coat that he had forgotten he had placed there the day before. She would feel her temper rising as she thought everyone was ready but when she turned around to pick up the toddler, she was lying on the floor, coat cast aside, sucking her thumb and refusing to budge.

'We're going to be late! Get up!!' she would yell as the toddler literally and figuratively dug her heels in. She would scoop her up, deafened by two-year old protests, and head out the door, and then our son would realise he had forgotten something. It was the same routine, and while she allowed more and more time each day to get ready and to try to keep the stress levels down, there was always something, always some kind of drama.

'I must be the worst mother in the world!' she would sigh to herself as they left the house, everybody stressed and nobody smiling. She would see other kids skipping towards the school gate while she carried the weight of a grumpy toddler and a ball of lead in her stomach. 'How come other mothers can manage, what is wrong with me?' she would say to me as we climbed into bed at night. It was her mantra and she practiced it daily and nightly. She would repeat over and over that she was a bad mother, she was not doing the right thing for the children, she was not able to stay calm and manage things lovingly. She thought she would ruin our kids and their chance later in life by her impatience and her anger and her exhaustion.

She was afraid of repeating the mistakes her parents had made with her. But aren't we all? She convinced herself of the negatives, and in so doing, blocked herself from seeing the positives. The way she could calmly soothe an upset or a child-size injustice, how she would relish her time reading to the kids in bed each night, sharing in their delight as they heard tales from other lands, and as they discussed ideas they heard in the stories. What if she had taken a step back each night to really examine what had happened that day. How she may have yelled at the children three times but hugged them twenty times. How she had said a cross word or barked a command five times but laughed out loud at their silly antics fifteen times. What if she had changed her mantra to a positive one by telling herself every night that she was a fantastic mother, she was the exact mother her children needed, that she was the most loving mother in the world? I believe by so doing she would have allowed the transgressions in emotions to be seen as invaluable lessons for her children, as a wonderful way to teach them about the world and their own emotions.

The perfect mother would never be able to teach her children the gift of forgiveness as she would never have to ask it of them. The perfect mother would not have prepared her children for the disappointment that comes hand-in-hand with a bad grade at school, or a failed entrance to university or a terrible boss who never gave praise. A friend who was mean or a moment in life that pulls out tears and strong emotions. The simple act of losing patience but then recovering, or yelling but then apologising, teaches children so much more than perfect balance. Perfect balance does not exist in the real world, but emotions do.

To me a perfect mother is one who can listen to their child and be their point of stability and security. Who can sympathise with their feelings but teach them how to move on. Who can react appropriately to their child's demands which sometimes means saying no. Who doesn't feel the need to constantly entertain their children, who values boredom for the gift that it is and who teaches their children that everything in life needs balance, and sometimes the parent needs to rebalance their own life by doing their own things and by putting themselves first. The perfect mother teaches resilience and independence and sometimes this comes through difficult moments with our children and not through perfectly orchestrated, picture-perfect moments of domestic bliss.

This is why the 'perfect mother' does not exist. God knew what he was doing when he created women.

I dread to think what it is like for parents who live day to day with social media. We luckily never had that added burden, but no wonder everyone is secretly miserable! Everyone nowadays holds themselves up to an even higher vision of perfection, falsely created by what they see on their social media accounts. The photos of perfectly turned out children smiling next to their relaxed and happy parents. Holiday destinations flashed around, or scenes of wonderful weekends spent together as a family. No-one sees the fight that occurred just before the photo was taken, the bribes it took to get the children to stand still for just long enough to take the photo. The tiredness felt by the parents because of a toddler who had been up five times during the previous night, or the absent husband who puts his arm quickly around his wife's shoulders for the photo but then removes it just as quickly once the photo is taken. It is too easy to fall for the untruths of the moments we see before us in these carefully selected and orchestrated snapshots placed not-so-casually on a social media account. I am so glad that was not our reality as young parents.

As I look at my wife now, as she takes her makeup off, I see how beautiful she is. I watch her curls unfold and fold up again as she passes the brush through them. I watch as she puts toothpaste on her toothbrush, never squeezing up the remaining paste to the top of the tube as I used to wish she would do. We had different habits, my wife and I, different idiosyncrasies I guess I would now call them. Little things that we would do that unintentionally annoyed the other. I used to like the taps to shine. I would polish them every day and yet every time I went into the bathroom there would be water marks on the tap again.

I remember we had quite a fight about it one day. It was silly looking back on it now, but I couldn't understand why she couldn't accommodate what I thought was a simple request, and she couldn't understand why I didn't let it go. They were taps.

They were due to get wet, and why did it matter if they were not sparkling clean all the time? She kept a very tidy house, and I must say I never had to worry about cleanliness, but instead of focusing on her good points, and the things she did to make my life easier, I chose that day to nitpick. I exploded what was an insignificant thing into something that I believed represented a total lack of concern for me and my needs.

How silly looking back, and if I could turn back time I would take that moment as an opportunity to thank her for all she did for us rather than focusing on what she didn't do. It took us a long time to come down from our high horses after that. It's easy to get up there but not always easy to come down. We chose not to talk about it anymore after that day but I could see that it hurt her far deeper than she let on.

So here she is now, as beautiful as ever, having one last look at herself in the mirror and what does she do but pick up the hand towel and wipe down the tap! 'Goodnight Darling' she says to the air as she turns around and turns out the bathroom light and heads towards the bed. I notice her wipe a tear from her eye as a small sob escapes from her mouth.

I watch her as she pulls back the covers and slowly climbs into her side of the bed. She picks up her tube of hand cream and rubs a dollop into her now-aging hands. Hands that have held our newborn babies, hands that have wiped away tears from faces freshly fallen off bicycles, hands that have protectively held together the broken hearts of teenagers. Who lovingly and shakily pinned the flower to our son's lapel as he prepared to walk down the aisle, who buttoned up our daughter's dress as she prepared to fly the nest to start her own life.

I couldn't have had the life I had without her. I loved her with all my heart but I never really knew how to say it. I assumed she knew, but assumptions can be dangerous and lead us into false beliefs.

As my wife snuggles down under the covers she picks up the

photo frame next to the bed that contains a photo of us on our wedding day. She kisses it and her eyes linger over it a moment before she places it back down carefully on the bedside table, her moist eyes shining in the lamplight. She reaches towards the lamp and turns it out.

We lie on our backs and I place my hand on hers. We weren't very affectionate during the day but at night we would lean towards each other for comfort. We allowed our vulnerabilities to come through as we lay safely tucked up in bed. Why we couldn't do that during the day I cannot figure out, but there is something about the tough face you have to show to the world while you think the world is looking that forces those vulnerabilities and sensibilities down and out of sight. It is the security and warmth of bed that seems to draw them back out again.

I remember when we met. She was working in her father's grocery store and as I walked in there to buy the apples my mother needed for dessert, I noticed her beauty. She was not what I would call a classic beauty, but the beauty on her inside clearly shone out for everyone to see. She had her hair tied up in the bouffant hair-style that was popular in those days, an apron firmly tied around her waist. She was helping a customer choose the best lemons and she didn't notice me enter the shop. When she finally looked up and saw me standing at the counter, she gave me the warmest smile and I was hooked. Here was the creature I had been look-ing for all my life and instead of finding her in a magazine or on the silver screen, she was standing right in front of me in all her unglamorous glory. What a vision she was! She walked over to the counter and said she would be with me shortly. She very kindly helped her customer count out coins from a frail hand, wished her a wonderful day and told her to mind her step on the way out. Then she turned to me.

All I could do was stammer something about needing apples and my mind went blank when she asked me what type. I just stared at her open mouthed and she laughed her tinkling laugh and gently asked me to follow her. I would have followed her to the ends of the earth but I found myself in front of a large pile of red and green apples. I asked for the green ones and was soon on my way home feeling a lightness in my step I hadn't experienced before. I suppose that is what it feels like when you give away your heart. I never knew mine had been so heavy.

I went back the next day and the next. Mother couldn't understand why I was so keen to suddenly help her with the groceries, but as she came with me one day, under great protests on my part, the penny dropped.

'Ask her out!' she whispered as her rounded elbow met with my side.

My mouth went dry, I mumbled my excuses and left. As I got outside I leant against the wall, one foot up behind me for support. I let out a huge sigh and silently berated myself for lost opportunities.

I went back the next day to buy some lettuce that I am certain Mother did not need, and there she was, my Venus, my beauty that I was too shy and nervous to reach out and touch. I took a deep breath. 'Come on, you can do this. COME ON!' I softly yelled to myself. Never had anything been so hard in all my life! With my stomach tossing and turning like a boat on a rough sea I quickly spat out 'I-would-like-one-lettuce-please-and-would-you-like-to-come-to-the-picture-show-with-me-this-Saturday.' Phew. It was done. And then I had to wait for what felt like forever as her eyes drifted off to the side to help her think. *What is taking her so long?!* I thought in a panic. I wanted to run as fast as I could out of that shop to never return. I think I stopped breathing as the room started to blur and my lungs involuntarily took in a huge gulp of air.

'I have something on this Saturday but I hear that there is a new James Bond film coming out next week. Why don't we go together next weekend?'

'YES!' I silently screamed, my insides doing my best impression of John Travolta in *Saturday Night Fever*. I tried to act a bit more mature on the outside as I smiled and said I would like that.

'Here's the lettuce. You don't have to pay for it. It's my treat as you are our best customer,' she said very kindly. I thanked her and took the lettuce with shaking hands. When I got outside I started to run, but this time not out of fear and a means of escape but because a wave of pure joy had taken over my body and I wanted to run and sing and scream and punch the air!

I ran through the front door bursting with the news I was about to share with Mother. She smiled as I handed over the lettuce and told her she had said yes. It was then that I realised I didn't even know her name, but it didn't matter. I had found my angel and I would simply ask her the next time I saw her.

We went on several dates after that and it didn't take long before we were engaged to be married. I had saved up all my money to buy her a ring, and while it wasn't much of a ring, I knew that she would appreciate it. I wrote to her father asking for a meeting. As I walked up to the house, I felt my stomach flipping and turning over again, but I said to myself that no matter what, I would marry that girl, and so as I took a deep breath and rang the doorbell, I focused on her becoming my wife.

It was over a glass of Scotch that the deal was done. What a funny tradition! As if the woman herself had no say in the matter. But there is also something very respectful in the tradition that nods to the role a father plays in his daughter's life.

Our wedding was a simple affair. We were young, way too young by today's standards, but when you are young you feel like love conquers all. We had thirty people celebrate with us and held our reception afterwards in the local pub. She wore a plain yet stylish pale blue dress and had tiny white flowers pinned to her hair. I wore a brown suit and matching tie and bought new shoes for the occasion. I had forgotten to wear them in and so my feet ached as we stood before the vicar in the local church to say our vows.

A friend had loaned us his car. An Austin-Healey Sprite. It

was decorated with empty tin cans and someone had written 'Just Married' across the back windscreen with lipstick. What a day that was! We felt on top of the world, a world full of hope and promise, like nothing bad could reach us up there!

I suppose time changes a relationship and as we settled into married life and learned we were to have a baby, routine installed itself and we fell into our daily rhythm. She was a wonderful mother to our newborn son but I could see she was a bit anxious. She told me one night that she never seemed to be able to get rid of that fine layer of nervousness that had installed itself in the pit of her stomach. She was never the best sleeper and her sleeping became even worse as she would lie awake at night keeping an ear out for that unmistakable newborn cry.

She had problems settling our son and he would cry for hours, quite often joined by his mother. I suppose this is when the guilt set in and it never really left her. Mother's guilt is such a terrible and unnecessary thing.

She turns over and I hear her breathing change as she falls asleep. She must be lonely now that I'm gone and I hope that she finds comfort in her dreams. I watch as her shoulders move up and down in time to her breathing and notice how her face has now relaxed and the tension lines around her eyes and her mouth have started to soften. I catch a glimpse of her glasses on the bedside table and they remind me of how much the children would laugh when my wife would make spaghetti for dinner. As she tipped the hot water into the colander in the sink, the steam from the hot spaghetti would fog up her glasses which would make the children laugh hysterically. How they managed to find it so funny each time it happened I will never know, but they sure did love it!

I loved my wife in so many ways and for so many things. I loved her with all my heart and could not imagine a life without her. I am so grateful to have found my courage the day I asked her out, as it was bravery and lettuce that brought us together. I feel such a regret now welling up inside me. I never really showed her how much I loved her. I suppose I did in my funny sort of a way, but sometimes it is best to say these things and not assume that one knows them.

As I continue to lie next to my wife, I am grateful for these last moments together. I want to savour them as I know they will be our last. As she continues to sleep peacefully next to me, I surround her with as much love as I possibly can, unable to physically hold her but knowing I can share my soul with her.

The morning has come now. It is time for me to leave. I lean over and delicately kiss her cheek and place my hand on her still-warm and sleepy head. 'Goodbye my darling,' I whisper in her ear. 'Thank you for a lifetime of happiness, a lifetime of sacrifice. A lifetime of always putting others before yourself. I hope you aren't lonely. I couldn't think of anything worse than you being lonely. Surround yourself with friends. You have been very loved in this life and deserve others to look after you for a change. I wish I had told you how much I love you. I wish with all my heart that I could hold you just one more time and tell you how much I truly and deeply love you. We have had our struggles and our difficult moments, but my life was so wonderful with you by my side. What I would give to feel your hands holding my face one more time, to see your beautiful smile as I walk through the door after a long day apart. To share a comment and a slice of toast with you as we read the Sunday paper in bed. How I long to smell your perfume just one last time as it lingers on my shirt after my quick peck of a kiss goodbye in the morning. How your face lights up with pure joy as our grandchildren run in the door to see their Nana and Pop. You are my everything my Sweetheart, the great love of my life, the one constant that never disappointed me but was always there for me. I have to be content now with the hope that you know this. Hope is all I have now for there is nothing more I can do as my time has run out.'

I lean over one more time and delicately kiss her mouth, her nose, her forehead. 'I love you,' I say with every ounce of my remaining strength. A light has appeared in the room now to counteract the sunlight starting to stream in through the window. The light is calling me and I want to walk towards it. I know I am safe and loved and protected by that light and that is where my heart and soul must now go.

I take one more long look at my sleeping love and whisper goodbye.

I thank you, dear reader, for taking this journey with me. For witnessing my learnings and goodbyes. And this is what I want to share with you. Take the time to be with your loved ones, laugh with your kids when you're feeling down, take that trip, have tea with your neighbour, start that business you were always too scared to start, but remember that we all end up here one day. Don't leave this life with regrets. Fill each day with love and happiness and surround yourself with blessings. Life, after all, is meant to be about joy.

And with these thoughts, I bid you goodbye.

Author's Note

I was cleaning my teeth one night, feeling sleepy and ready to get into bed when Mr Jones jumped into my head. One minute I was zoning out and the next minute I was wide awake seeing a life flash before my eyes. In the space of what felt like ten seconds I suddenly felt that I knew the man who had entered my head, and I could feel the urgency with which he presented me his story. While I never met him in the flesh, I knew I had been chosen to tell his story and to spread the message that many of us need to hear.

With tears rolling down my cheeks and a very surprised husband looking on, I picked up my phone and started furiously typing into it. The feelings and emotions were pouring through me and I had to get the visions in my head noted down. I had seen the beginning and the end, and I knew that the rest of the story would come to me as I wrote.

Within two months the story was complete, which took me by surprise as, having young children, I do not get a lot of time to write.

I was sad to say goodbye to Mr Jones when the writing process was complete but now his story is immortalised in print and I hope I have done it justice.

Acknowledgements

This book has come about because of a journey and this journey would not have been possible without the loving and inspired support of so many people.

I would like to firstly thank my husband and my sons who have supported and encouraged my writing and have never lost faith in my vision.

To my parents for always encouraging reading and for allowing my imagination to blossom. A particular thank you goes to my mother and her incredible storytelling abilities. Through her example I learned to wow people with my words.

Thank you to my aunt who reads faster than anyone in history and who lent me her years of editing skills to get this book ready for reading.

Thank you to Debra Moffitt who has helped awaken the writer in me, for teaching me to trust my intuition and how to tap into it.

To my friends who have supported me from up close and afar, as I stepped on to the path I was always supposed to take.

And finally, to my faith and courage. Without these two traits my words would never have found paper.

READING GROUP QUESTIONS

1. What do you think the main message of the book is?
2. The story raises the idea that we should all strive to live the life of our dreams rather than the 'safe' option. What do you think about that message? Is risk necessary to living a dream life and if yes, what are the risks?
3. Do you believe societal and parental expectations play too strong a role in the life path that people choose?
4. Mr Jones acknowledges that he treated his daughter differently to his son. In what ways did this manifest and why do you think these differences existed?
5. Forgiveness is an important theme in this book. Should we always forgive people who do us 'wrong'? Why or why not? What is the true benefit of forgiveness?
6. Mr Jones describes the relationship he had with his parents as well as the relationship he had with his own children. How do you think the way he was parented affected the way he parented his son and daughter?
7. Mr Jones recounts the story of working with a very difficult boss. Despite this experience being extremely stressful for him, what did he gain from this relationship and situation?
8. This book explores the many relationships that Mr Jones has through out his life. Which story had the biggest impact on you and why?